NARUTO

SASUKE'S STORY

[S U N R I S E]

Masashi Kishimoto
Shin Towada

First published in Japan in 2015 by SHUEISHA Inc., Tokyo.
English translation rights arranged by SHUEISHA Inc.

Cover and interior design by Shawn Carrico

Translation by Jocelyne Allen

Published by
VIZ Media, LLC
P.O. Box 77010
San Francisco, CA 94107

www.viz.com

Library of Congress Cataloging-in-Publication data has been applied for.

Printed in the U.S.A.

First printing, March 2017

SASUKE'S STORY

[SUNRISE]

ORIGINAL STORY BY

Masashi Kishimoto

WRITTEN BY

Shin Towada

TRANSLATED BY

Jocelyne Allen

Prologue 007

1 Dark clouds appearing in a world of change 011

2 Shadow of the past revived by lightning 061

3 Ostentatious welcome, roar of grief 101

CONTENTS

4 Where the red eyes gaze 137

Epilogue 163

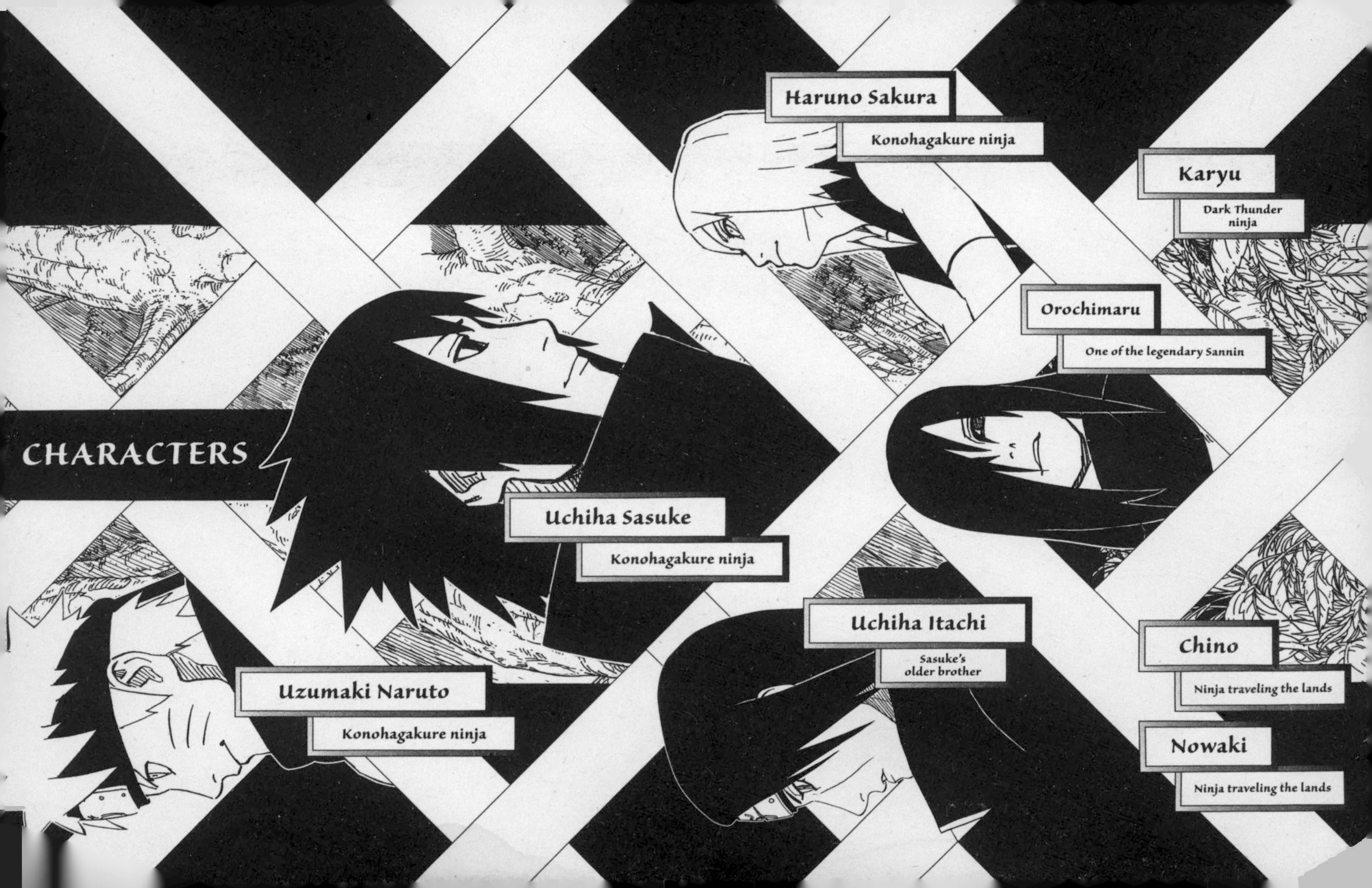
CHARACTERS
Uzumaki Naruto
Konohagakure ninja
Uchiha Sasuke
Konohagakure ninja
Haruno Sakura
Konohagakure ninja
Uchiha Itachi
Sasuke's older brother
Orochimaru
One of the legendary Sannin
Karyu
Dark Thunder ninja
Chino
Ninja traveling the lands
Nowaki
Ninja traveling the lands

Prologue

PROLOGUE

I was alone and starved of love, a child spurred on by hatred. I took a different path from my friend, who knew pain similar to my own. I chose a path of further loneliness.

Connections give rise to the warmth of emotion, and these occasionally flashed brightly, exposing my own weakness in the harsh light of day. My body was enveloped in darkness; I turned my back to the light, my heart stained black with hatred.

To get revenge on my older brother, Itachi, who killed my clan, my family. To get revenge on Konoha for pinning all their crimes on Itachi, for using him. To bring about a revolution in this world and build a world without mistakes with my own power.

I can't just let you go!!

And there, my only friend standing in my way. A shinobi who knows my pain. Relentlessly honest, he is a man who does not stray from his word.

I brushed him off any number of times, even tried to take his life. And yet he did not give up, he did not abandon me; he desperately reached out to me, locked onto me. And this man—the man I tried so hard to sever my relationship with—he pulled me out of my solitude.

I lost.

I remember the dazzling light of the morning sun in the Valley of the End—although I had chosen the place with the intent of a final, decisive battle—the pain we shared in our hearts, the warm tears on my cheeks. I will never forget.

Naruto. My friend. He said, *What I wanna do is get all shinobi to cooperate with each other! Including you, of course!*

I am in Naruto's world. I am blessed to exist.

His was like the warmth I once got from my family. It made me feel that I truly existed in this world. The connections with my family, the love.

Revenge had supported me. At the same time, it had eaten away at me. Hatred raced through my body like a poison, and killed all other human emotion. And when I was in that state, he lit the fire in my heart once more.

I stepped onto a new path. A path leading from the past to the future. It is not an even path, however. This world still contains all kinds of pain.

Sharingan in my right eye, rinnegan in my left.

The future reflected in these eyes that once stared into darkness...

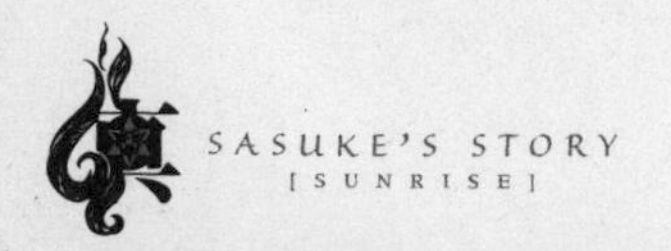

1 Dark clouds appearing in a world of change

CHAPTER 1

Dark clouds appearing in a world of change

1

"Give my best regards to the Lord Raikage as well."

The vast ocean was veiled in white mist. Not particularly good for visibility, but the women were accustomed to fog; they could see quite well, even in these conditions.

Enclosed on all four sides by the ocean, The Land of Water, one of the lands known as the five great ninja nations, was also home to the village of Kirigakure. The days when Kirigakure was known as the Village of the Bloody Mist and the origin of Akatsuki were in the distant past. Yagura, the fourth Mizukage, had dirtied his hands with all sorts of evil, but the genjutsu cast on him had been released by the late Ao's byakugan, and with Terumi Mei's assumption of the office of Fifth Mizukage, the situation in Kirigakure was steadily improving.

And then, the Fourth Great Ninja War changed the world completely. The constantly quarrelling five great ninja lands had joined hands and come through the terrible battles together, becoming war comrades. Even after the Great War, they had worked together to overcome the difficulties that arose to shake the world. Many lives had been sacrificed in the war, and those who survived lived with great sadness, but the things gained were also great.

"Please be thorough in your duties in the joint training between Kirigakure and Kumogakure!" Chojuro—carrying the large twinsword Hiramekarei that was proof that he was one of the Seven Ninja Swordsmen—called to the ninja preparing to sail away.

The surf pounded against the port. A ship large enough to carry a hundred people was currently moored there, in this critical location for the Land of Water, surrounded by the sea as the country was.

Some people had kicked up a fuss when the decision was made to train together with another village, but still the feeling of friendship was actually quite strong. The fact that they had exchanges like this with other lands was due in large part to Uzumaki Naruto and the many incredible things he had accomplished during the Fourth Great Ninja War. His hope was that ninja would come together to create a world without war.

"These sorts of experiences will also be good for the future of Kirigakure," the Mizukage remarked to the squad leader in charge of the joint training group.

"Yes, ma'am! We will be *bold. Made* for this mission, we will build a basis for friendship with other nations!" The squad leader responded sincerely to this hope of the Mizukage.

But she reacted with a gasp. *Old maid?!*

Utterly ignorant of the Mizukage's state of upset, Chojuro said to the squad leader, "The Lord Raikage is *hard on both self and others at times*. But he is a firm and brave man. He gives his all to everything he does. Also, this time of year, powerful typhoons

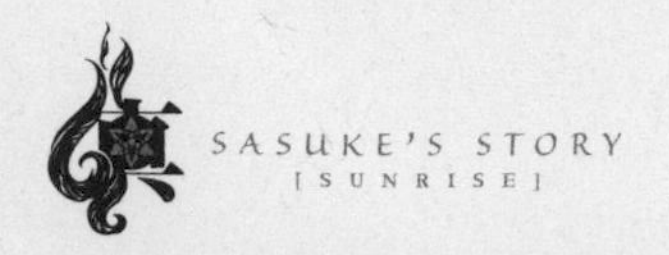

often form around the islands neighboring the Land of Water, so please do not a*ct rash*ly. Keep an eye out for them."

"Ha ha! So now you worry about other people now, hm, Chojuro? Better off *her*ding cats."

Old maid, hard on both self and others at times...Trash her?!

As Chojuro and the others chatted cheerfully, the look on the Mizukage's face grew grim, and an ominous aura rose up around her.

Noticing her silence, Chojuro cocked his head curiously to one side and looked at her. "Lady Mizukage, is something the matter?"

She exhaled a long breath and collected her scattered nerves. "I just remembered things with Ao... If he were here..."

"Oh, Ao... I wish he could see me now too." Chojuro had apparently taken her statement to mean she wanted to show off the now-grown Chojuro to Ao.

Rather than correcting him, the Mizukage smiled, and brought their conversations together with a "Truly."

"All right, then! We'll be off!" a ninja on the ship called, now that all members were aboard; the ship slowly left the port.

"The five great nations hated each other so much, and now we can join hands like this," Chojuro murmured, deeply moved, as they watched it sail off in a mist of sea spray. "It's simply incredible, isn't it?"

"Yes, it really is." The Mizukage felt something more than this, than how Chojuro felt the transformation of this changing world in his own way. She was one of the shinobi who had lived through the dark days of Kirigakure. She had fought, drenched in the blood of others, in her own blood, for the sake of the village.

Back then, if a ninja was determined to be a burden, they were simply thrown to the wolves. It had indeed been a time when everything was suspect, when they had lost sight of what they were living for, what they believed in, as if they had been in a thick fog. That environment had produced, among others, Momochi Zabuza, feared as a demon; Haku of the Yuki clan, toyed with by the sad destiny of kekkei genkai; and Hoshigaki Kisame, who bore the darkness of Kirigakure alone—so-called "evil" ninja. As a ninja from the same village, from the same era, however, the Mizukage secretly had complicated feelings about calling them evil.

With the tensions among the five great nations easing, and thus, fewer and fewer battles, this world, formerly centered around fighting, was now changing from its foundations. Which meant that both ninja and average citizens also needed to change to adapt to these new times. But not everyone could accept this. There were inevitably going to be people who rejected and despised the idea of this change, who would try to destroy this new world.

In her struggle to undo the negative inheritance left by the former Mizukage and Kirigakure's own history, the current Mizukage, Mei, was coming up against all kinds of difficulties, so she knew. Change was no simple matter.

The ship bound for the Land of Lightning had become a shadow in the distance in the blink of an eye. The Mizukage strained her eyes to follow the hazy ship disappearing into the white mist.

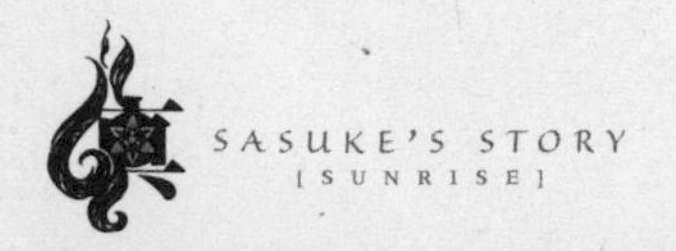

CHAPTER 1

∞

"It got cloudy all of a sudden."

The Kirigakure ninja keeping watch on the deck of the ship looked up at the sky. It had been a day since the ship set out from the port in the Land of Water toward the Land of Lightning. After they slipped through the white fog, they had been blessed with good weather, but abruptly, black clouds started gathering above them. The wind blew against her cheeks, and the calm face of the ocean began to change.

"A storm might be coming." The watch ninja took a step to go and report to the people inside. But she felt eyes on her somehow. Unconsciously, she turned in that direction and saw a small boat in the ocean, in the breaks between the waves. "A fishing boat?"

Aboard the vessel were several people dressed like fishermen in straw raincoats and woven *amigasa* hats. But therc were many islands of all sizes in this area, and more than a few of their residents made their living fishing. There was no need to be particularly concerned. Or so she thought, but the boat was gradually heading toward them.

"Hey! You're going to hit us!" she called out a warning, but the boat didn't show any signs of stopping. "Hey!" The watch ninja leaned over from the ship, grabbed her forehead protector with the Kirigakure crest on it, and held it up. Perhaps there came through in this a boast that they were ninja of Kirigakure, an unconscious arrogance that fishermen like them couldn't do anything about it.

One of the people in the boat stood up. Woven hat deep over

their eyes. Fingers grasping the edge, slowly lifting it. The hidden chin, the mouth, the nose were revealed, and then...

The instant she saw the eyes, the watch ninja fell down.

"H-hey! What's wrong?!" The eyes of the other ninja on deck grew wide at their comrade suddenly dropping to the deck after calling out a warning to the small boat ahead of them. But before any of them could race over to her side, they sensed an abnormal aura.

"Wh-who's there?!"

The mysterious person, face covered by the woven hat, landed soundlessly, alone, on the deck of the ship. From the way they carried themselves, there was no doubt they were a ninja.

Hearing the commotion, the squad leader came running up. "Seize them!"

The ninja of Kirigakure began to weave signs to capture and eliminate the intruder. They were on the water; given the number of Water Style users in Kirigakure, they should have had the upper hand.

However, the intruder calmly lifted the edge of the hat again.

"Wha—!!"

Young ninja with promising futures, veteran shinobi who had lived through the time known as the Village of the Bloody Mist and survived the Fourth Great Ninja War, all of them crumpled on the spot, unable to do anything against this lone ninja opponent.

CHAPTER 1

∞

"They're late."

The ninja of Kumogakure grumbled, waiting in the drizzling rain to greet the ninja of Kirigakure at the port in the Land of Lightning. The scheduled arrival time was long past, and no message had come to say the ship would be late.

"The Lord Raikage's going to lose it if they're too late."

Their straightforward, short-tempered Raikage. If they kept him waiting too long, he would erupt in anger; he might very well bring the lightning of his name down on them.

"Maybe the weather's not working with them. There's nowhere out on the ocean to get out of the rain, after all."

"But they could at least send a messenger hawk from the ship, right? It'd make it easier for us to report to up high too, if they'd send a little note saying they're late."

"That's true, but..."

The wind brushed against the cheeks of the increasingly wetter Kumogakure ninja. After considering again the possibility that their arrival could be even further delayed, they decided to send a messenger to Kumogakure.

"Hey, wait. Is that it there?"

A ship had finally appeared on the horizon.

"So they finally show up, huh?"

The ship bore the mark of Kirigakure; it was clearly the one they were waiting for.

"It's kind of really quiet, huh?"

There was no one on the deck; they couldn't see any Kirigakure ninja. Perhaps they had gone into the cabin to avoid the rain.

As the ship approached, the wind and rain grew more intense. Almost as if bringing something sinister.

"Welcome to the Land of Lightning!" the Kumogakure representative called out, as the ship reached the shore.

There was no response from inside. Thinking this suspicious, the Kumogakure ninja looked at each other.

"Welcome!" she shouted again, her voice tense.

Finally, someone appeared from within the ship. A ninja wearing a woven hat. This ninja glanced down at the representative who had called out to welcome the ship.

"...Oh..." The representative swayed, and then collapsed on the rain-slick port.

"Wh-what's wrong?!"

The Kumogakure ninja were bewildered by this sudden event.

The ninja in the hat jumped down from the ship and tossed the hat away, revealing what had been hidden beneath it.

"Th-those eyes?!"

Crimson eyes glowing eerily in the rain. Not one of the Kumogakure ninja escaped being caught in their gaze.

"Crap, ocular jutsu..."

Merely upon seeing that red glow, the ninja of Kumogakure lost all their strength and fell to the ground.

"That was wonderful." Red Eyes' comrades leaped down from the ship after watching the scene play out.

"Put them in the ship," Red Eyes instructed, and the other ninja nodded.

The Kirigakure ninja were already inside the ship, flat on their backs, not moving so much as a muscle.

While the others hauled the Kumogakure shinobi up, Red Eyes picked up the woven hat and put it back on. The weather grew increasingly rough, and the black clouds, stirred up by the wind, twisted like a giant snake.

"We got them all!" one ninja shouted, and Red Eyes leapt up back onto the ship.

A bolt of lightning raced across a sky rumbling with thunder.

"We'll dye it all red."

I will not allow this peace.

2

The woods were thick. Ivy twined around fat trunks, down to the roots of mossy trees, erasing the border between tree and earth. This particular tree that stretched its branches to the heavens, seeking the light of the sun, was hundreds of years old. But beyond it were young buds not yet grown.

Someone was looking down on it all. The left eye that barely peeked out from the hair hanging across his face was the supreme rinnegan. At first glance, the right looked to be a normal eye, but it housed the sharingan, the kekkei genkai of the Uchiha clan. The man's name was Uchiha Sasuke.

At the top of the massive tree, Sasuke looked out at the view in all directions. He had made it through the Fourth Great Ninja War and come back a shinobi of Konoha once more. However, rather than staying in the village, he had set out on a journey.

I want to know how this ninja world—how the world looks to me now.

He had been traveling for several years, and had seen things he probably wouldn't have noticed when he was steeped in darkness. There had also been times when he looked back gently on the past he had tried to break free of. There were moments when he remembered his friends. He saw with his own eyes the scars of the war; he touched on people's sadness, and felt the futility of revenge.

In the past, Sasuke had endured the pain and suffering of having his family and his clan taken from him with the powerful medicine of revenge. But in the depth of that darkness, he had become confused about what path to go down. He had lost sight of what was important. It had taken a very long time to be able to understand and accept that, but Sasuke truly felt it now.

He felt the changes in the world as well. The five Kage had moved to make major wars disappear, and maintain peace and order. Once, the power of the ninja was used to protect their own countries, and to invade and attack other nations. Now, it was being made use of to develop equipment that did not require chakra to instantly transmit information, to maintain medical facilities, to actively communicate with other nations, and to enhance distribution systems, among other things. The world was stepping into a new age of growth.

Which was exactly why he could not overlook one particular issue.

Otsutsuki Kaguya.

The woman who had taken in her mouth the fruit of the Divine Tree—said to be forbidden—gained chakra, and brought

calm to a turbulent world. But she had been consumed by the immense power, and after a time when she ran wild, her own children, Hamura and Hagoromo, had sealed her away.

That very Kaguya had come back to this world, and Sasuke had, along with his comrades in Team 7 and Uchiha Obito, sealed her away once more. Once the threat that had rocked the world had passed, people rejoiced, but something about it bothered Sasuke.

Through Black Zetsu's secret maneuvering to bring her back, Kaguya had linked the people she cast Infinite Tsukiyomi on to the roots of the Divine Tree, transforming them over many years into her personal soldiers. The end result was the army of White Zetsu.

Formerly known as the Rabbit Goddess, Kaguya changed somehow after she had freed the world from conflict, so the people connected to the Divine Tree also came after the peace she brought about. Why, in a world where fighting was supposed to have ended, was there a need to use the Infinite Tsukiyomi on people and turn them into soldiers? To play cruelly with those who had power, to control human beings with fear; a number of reasons came to mind, but Sasuke could see no clear answer.

He was chasing after the traces Kaguya had left behind to clear away his doubts, but his opponent was the progenitor of chakra. Sasuke might have had the rinnegan, but picking up her trail was no easy feat.

"Mm?" Sensing an aura, he looked toward the southwest. When he squinted, he could see something flying in his direction. At first glance, it was a small bird flapping its wings, but circulating in that bird was not blood, but ink and text brought to life by chakra.

Sasuke quickly pulled out a scroll, and the bird flew toward it as if called. Konoha ninja Sai's Art of Cartoon Beast Mimicry. The figure of the bird disappeared, and in its place, text spread out on the open scroll.

Thinking that he needed to have a more diverse view of the world in order to know Kaguya, Sasuke had recently deliberately begun communicating with Konoha more often, asking them to send him information on the state of the village and of the world.

He turned his gaze to the words on the page, thinking it was one of those missives, but his brow furrowed at the content. "This..."

It was a message from the current Hokage, Hatake Kakashi. Apparently, a large number of ninja from Kirigakure and Kumogakure had suddenly disappeared. There was no sign of a fight, and information was limited, so the Hokage was asking him to contact Konoha if he found anything suspicious that might have been related to the incident.

"More than a hundred ninja suddenly vanish?"

If a person was behind it, it was possible that they were a genjutsu user. In which case, it would be best for Sasuke, with his superior ocular jutsu, to respond. If he used the sharingan, he might be able to see what other ninja couldn't.

At the top of the tree he had climbed to check his direction, Sasuke looked around once more with those eyes. Several clouds of white smoke puffed up into the air beyond the forest he was perched in. Not from fires, though. It was steam. He was that close to Yugakure, a village where hot springs welled up out of

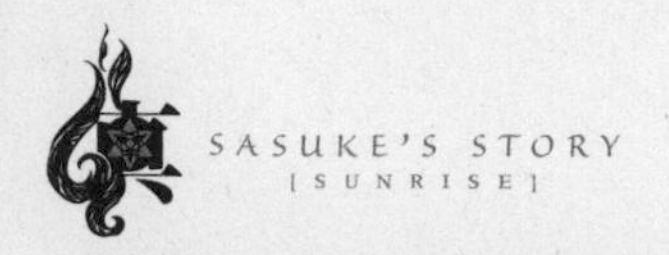

the earth, often used as a hot-spring resort. It was in the Land of Steam, which was not far from the Land of Lightning, and ships always departed from there to the Land of Water.

"Maybe I'll head for the Land of Lightning, then." Given that he could reach it via a land route, Sasuke first set his sights on the Land of Lightning, and dropped back down into the forest.

∞

Until around the time the sun was setting, Sasuke charged forward silently, without resting, racing through a bamboo thicket. It was hard to jump through the supple, elastic bamboo the way he did with trees. As he moved across ground littered with bamboo leaves to quickly make his way out of the grove, Sasuke thought about the situation.

He was still in the Land of Steam. He wanted to be in the neighboring Land of Frost by the time the date changed, and then in the Land of Lightning and the village of Kumogakure the following day.

Abruptly, a small settlement came into his field of view. It was the sort of country village you'd see anywhere, but he unconsciously came to a stop.

There was not a single light in the village.

Although the sun had set, it was too early for everyone to have gone to sleep. And he had also just heard about the disappearance of a large number of ninja.

Sasuke closed his eyes for a moment and focused his power in his right eye. When he opened his eyelids, the eye was dyed red, three *tomoe* marks visible in it. Sharingan.

He looked at the village with that eye. There were indeed people inside the houses, which made ample use of the surrounding bamboo in their construction. But all of them were still like they were holding their breath. Almost as though they were afraid of something.

His curiosity piqued, Sasuke took a step toward the village.

"So you show yourself! You fallen Dark Thundeeeeerrrr!" Someone leapt out with a great deal of force from beneath the bamboo leaves.

Sasuke looked in that direction to find a balding old man, all skin and bones, charging at him, bamboo spear in hand. His movements were not quick, and he wasn't strong; he seemed to be a normal person with no connection with the ninja arts.

Sasuke jumped backward and lightly dodged. But in the spot where he landed, he felt chakra behind him.

"Water Release: Rain Barrage!" The high-pitched voice of a young girl rang out, and countless tiny pellets of water like the icing sugar on a sweet cake flew at him.

Sasuke wove signs, took a breath, and brought a finger to his mouth. *Fire Style: Great Fireball Technique!*

Fire Style was the specialty of the Uchihas. The flames he released enveloped the water pellets of his opponent, evaporating them instantly.

"What?! Water Style can be done in by Fire Style?!" his opponent shouted, upon seeing her own technique disappear without ever touching Sasuke. He looked over and saw a short girl with a childish face standing there.

"Chino, get back!" Now a brawny man appeared, as if to push the girl "Chino" back. Kunai at the ready, he tossed it at

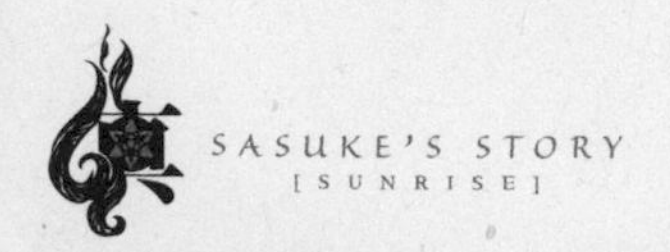

Sasuke, the tip aiming straight at his heart.

It stabbed into the bamboo behind him. *Rrrrrip!* The oversized grass exploded backward.

"Wind's changing nature, hm?" Sasuke noted. The kunai, cloaked in wind chakra, had expanded the air inside the node of the bamboo and ruptured it.

"Hey! You youngsters, what are you at?! Hurry up and take him down!" the old man shouted.

"Whaaaat?! No one told me he was this strong!" Chino frowned and stared at Sasuke. And then she gasped and pointed at his eye. "No! No way! Look, Nowaki! That eye...the sharingan!"

A surprised look rose up on the face of the large man, who was apparently Nowaki. "Is that real?"

"You listen, you spineless brats! You're gonna be like that, then I'll do it! Dark Thunder, I'll get vengeance for my daughterr!" Clutching his bamboo lance, the old man charged once more.

Sasuke didn't have a chance to even ask what was going on; in any case, he had no choice. "Hah!" He pushed out a hard breath, and took his sword in hand.

"Diiiiiiiieeee!" The old man pushed the bamboo lance forward.

Sasuke easily cut the end of it off. With incredible speed, he then sliced the lance into thin rounds up to the old man's hand, before bringing the tip of his sword up against the old man's windpipe. Sasuke pressed the blade against his throat as if to make him keenly aware of the cold sensation of the sword.

"Ee, eeep." The bamboo, chopped down to a single joint, fell from the old man's hand. Droplets of sweat popped up on his dry skin and fell to the ground.

"Ah, ah, w-wait, brother! Boss! Handsome! Manly! Don't kill the old man!" Panicked, Chino came at Sasuke as if to calm him.

Not responding to this, Sasuke said to the old man, "You've got the wrong idea."

"Hah, hah..."

"I don't know this Dark Thunder."

"Eee, eee..." Sasuke's words didn't seem to make it into the old man's ears; he kept breathing shallowly, trembling with fear. They wouldn't get anywhere like this.

Sasuke moved the blade of his sword the tiniest bit away from the old man's throat. "I am not Dark Thunder."

"What?"

"That's the first time I've heard the name." Sasuke lowered his sword, and the old man crumpled to his knees on the spot.

Meanwhile, Chino and Nowaki looked at each other.

"Iou! He says it's a mistake!" Chino shouted.

But the old man Iou moaned, "Shut up! This isn't the time for that! My heart, ah! My heart huuuurts!" Released from the terror of death, Iou's body responded with intense heart palpitations. He pressed a hand to his chest, and desperately sucked in air.

"Sorry. That was a terrible mistake for us to have made." Unlike Iou, Nowaki seemed sincerely apologetic.

"Although I feel like we would have been the ones to be killed if the fighting continued, I am sorry," Chino added, clapping both hands together in a gesture of contrition. "C'mon, Iou!

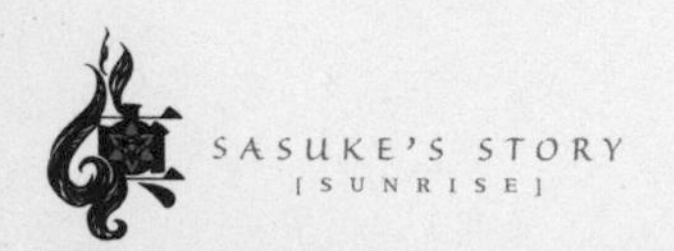

You say sorry, too!"

Still on the ground, Iou turned his face away. "Hmph! It's his fault for coming through Takeno at a time like this!" he cursed.

"Oooh, damned old man!"

"What did you say?!" Spurred on by Chino's words, Iou tried to stand up, but he quickly sat down hard again. Apparently, he had thrown his back out as well. He pounded the ground in vexation. "Ngh! And I thought for sure we'd settle things with the Dark Thunder gang today!"

"Exactly what is this Dark Thunder gang?" Iou had said he was going to get revenge for his daughter. There was no doubt something was happening here.

"Um, that story's a long one. ...Iou, let's go home for now. We have to explain things to the man here."

Like a stubborn child, Iou turned his face away. Chino grumbled an exasperated "Come onnnnnn," and then signaled Nowaki with her eyes.

"We're going back now, Iou." Nowaki hauled Iou up off the ground.

"Hngh!" the old man cried.

Nowaki started to walk toward the village, and Chino followed, hands clasped behind her head. Sasuke stared at their backs; Chino looked back to urge him on. "Hurry up!"

"This looks like it's going to be a hassle," Sasuke murmured as he moved to follow the three. But then he sensed eyes on him and whirled around.

Sasuke surveyed the scene, but there was only the bamboo forest spreading out before his eyes. It was quiet, no sign of any beast.

"Brother, what's the matter?" Chino called out, concerned.

Sasuke looked the bamboo thicket over once more before following after her.

∞

They brought him to Iou's house. Apparently, Iou was the mayor of this Takeno, and his home was remarkably large. Inside were all kinds of items made of bamboo, from everyday accessories to children's toys.

"So, like, Takeno apparently sells these bamboo crafts to make a living." Chino showed Sasuke the bamboo wicker baskets, skewers, and fishing rods, among other items off to one side.

"Don't go touching things!" Iou snatched a skewer from her with a snarl, but Chino wasn't put off in the least; she picked up a bamboo dragonfly and set it flying through the room. Unfortunately, it looked like it was going to land on top of Sasuke's head, but he caught it before it did, and held it up in front of him.

"I guess they sell all these in Yugakure. There's a lot of tourists there," Chino noted. "But the prices are too low, so they barely make anything off them."

"Quiet, you!" Iou roared instantly.

Yugakure was the rare ninja village that was also a tourist destination. And judging from the piled-up baskets and the large number of skewers in the work area, there seemed to indeed be a demand for the items, but life was apparently still hard in this village.

"Actually, me and Nowaki performed in Yugakure a little earlier."

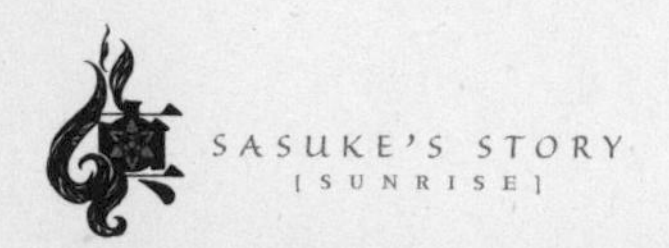

"Performed?" Sasuke raised an eyebrow.

"We're shinobi has-beens, traveling performers. We made some real coin in that onsen town. You can really clean up in entertainment there." Chino breathed out, and soap bubbles appeared, one after another. For a shinobi, it wasn't much of a trick, but it was probably well received by the average person. "So. We were heading off to a different area when we came through Takeno, okay? We stopped at the store for food, and this old man grabbed onto us. He begged us to help him get revenge, and then cried all over us."

They were finally getting to the subject at hand. As if compelled by Chino's story, Iou shouted, "It's all because of Dark Thunder! They're a heartless, soulless, evil organization! They come after tiny villages and pillage them! They kill people for sport! A few months ago, they came after the village my daughter married into...and they killed everyone!"

So that's why he was talking about revenge.

Perhaps remembering his daughter, tears sprang up in Iou's eyes. "We weren't blessed with children, and then after we got old, finally, my sweet baby girl! She got married last spring. She was going to have a baby soon!"

Seemingly unable to put his feelings into words any further, Iou gritted his teeth like he was trying to hold back his tears.

"He said his daughter was killed and his wife took sick from the shock of it and died," Chino finished.

Tragedy begets tragedy, and now all only Iou was left. It was a terrible situation—no wonder he had been driven to vengeance.

Having silently listened thus far, Nowaki looked pityingly at

Iou. "Apparently, the people of this area fear this Dark Thunder and live their lives in dread. Look at the windows."

When Sasuke did as instructed, he saw that blackout curtains hung over the windows so that no light leaked out. The people in the other houses likely had the same setup.

So that's why they had lain in wait, and tried to take down the Dark Thunder group.

"Now, you! You're strong, right! Please! Help me!" Iou roughly wiped his eyes with the back of his hand as he asked Sasuke for his help, almost throwing himself forward.

"Whaat? Isn't that a bit too selfish?" Chino sounded exasperated.

"Shut up!" Iou roared at her, and kept going without a pause. "I apologize for before!" He threw his head down in a deep bow, and then didn't move to bring it up again. Was he planning to keep bowing until Sasuke said yes?

Unable to just stand by and watch, Nowaki lowered his voice and said, "I'm not with Iou or anything, but actually, the leader of this Dark Thunder group is apparently saying his master is Uchiha Sasuke. And he's broadcasting it to the world."

"What did you say?" Sasuke unconsciously furrowed his brow at the sudden appearance of his own name in the conversation.

"That's you, right? Uchiha Sasuke. I guess he really looks up to you or something."

Unlike Iou, Chino and Nowaki had an understanding of ninja. And they were traveling performers. They would be privy to information as they journeyed around the world. It was precisely because of this that they had guessed who he was right away, once they saw his sharingan.

Sasuke had never heard of anyone calling themselves Dark Thunder. He was naturally annoyed at someone using his name however they pleased, but more than that, the fact that people out in the world doing evil were openly respectful of him shot a shadow of gloom into his heart. The shadow was dark and heavy.

"That's that, then," Sasuke murmured, slowly. Now that his name had been brought into it, he couldn't say it had nothing to do with him.

And it was a fact that the Dark Thunder group was violent, with many victims, and this village was exposed to that terror. The disappearance of a large number of ninja concerned him too, but he couldn't exactly walk away from this village. The reason Sasuke was on this journey was also to atone to the world, after all.

"Huh? You're gonna help?" Apparently, Chino didn't think Sasuke would help them. She looked at him with wide eyes. "I figured you'd say 'not my problem,' or 'fix it yourselves,' and then flip the table before taking off."

First of all, he would never flip a table, but the old Sasuke probably would have indeed said that. To begin with, the old him would have quickly passed through this village, and headed straight for the Land of Lightning.

"So you'll do it! You *are* the man I thought you were!" Iou raised his head, and a broad grin spread across his face. The change in his attitude was whiplash inducing.

Seeing Iou like this brought another person to mind. Tazuna, the bridge-builder from the Land of Waves. Tazuna had struggled against various obstacles to build his bridge, and he had the same audacity and quick-changing attitude. Maybe it was a special characteristic of this generation.

But the paths the two men had gone down were exactly opposite. Even after his loved one had been killed, Tazuna risked his life to fight for the future of the land, while Iou was spurred by hatred to see the power of vengeance.

"At any rate, that's enough for today, right? It doesn't seem like the Dark Thunder Group is gonna show. Let us rest." Chino made a show of yawning hugely.

"I s'pose. There's rooms here. Use 'em if you want. ...And if they do come, I'm really counting on you," Iou said, as if to drive the point home. His eyes showed that he was certain that this village was going to be attacked. And deeper in those eyes was a darkness that sought punishment for Dark Thunder for killing his daughter.

Even if Sasuke helped to resolve this incident, he had no intention of lending a hand to revenge. Although Iou likely wouldn't accept that. Instead of answering the old man, Sasuke went into the room he had been given.

∞

"Huh? Say that one more tiiiime."

A small village nestled in the mountains. But there were no longer any villagers in it. Destroyed houses, people cruelly forced to breathe their last. Only the beasts that caught the scent of blood were lively.

Inside a ruined house, the man sitting on the table and tossing a ball at the wall turned up the corners of his mouth at his

subordinate's words. Bluish-purple hair tied back loosely, pale lips. Only his eyes glittered and shone.

"Yes sir! Not long after the sun had set, when we went to scout out Takeno, there was a man using the sharingan! Lord Karyu, it was most likely Uchiha Sasuke!"

The ball hit the wall and bounced off the blood-soaked floor next to a corpse, and then returned to the man's—to Karyu's—hand.

"Uchiha Sasuke. The sole survivor of the proud Uchiha clan. So he's in Takeno..." Kaguya chuckled softly and jumped down from the table before throwing the ball up against the wall once more.

Thuk! There was a loud explosion, and the subordinate involuntarily plugged his ears and closed his eyes. When he opened them again, there was a large hole in the wall, and Karyu had stepped through it and gone outside.

Looking up at the moon hidden among the clouds, Karyu stretched out his hands. "My heart's teacher, the man who showed the world the wonder of kekkei genkai, Uchiha Sasuke... that I would get the chance to kill him!" A look of delight came across his face, and he shouted to his subordinates on standby, "All of you, get to work! Just the right time for Takeno... smash it all to pieces!"

3

The massive A-un gates connecting the village with the outside world were closed now, as if to escape the darkness of night; the enormous rock wall with the faces of the six generations of Hokage carved into it was quietly illuminated by the light of the moon spilling through the clouds.

Ancient even among the ninja villages, the Land of Fire's Konohagakure. This village, which had once taken catastrophic damage from Akatsuki's Pain, now shone even more brightly than it had in the past, and the population, which dropped during the Fourth Great Ninja War, was gradually recovering. Everything appeared to be going well, but every era inevitably had its trials.

"Hmm. This is actually a tough one."

The Hokage's office.

Looking over the letters that had arrived from Kirigakure and Kumogakure, the sixth Hokage, Kakashi, sighed. The missing shinobi were master hands. And with the ninja of Kirigakure, a hundred shinobi had disappeared all at once, together with a ship.

According to Kumogakure, someone who had seen the Kirigakure ship in the ocean near the port in the Land of Lightning. In which case, it was possible that the ship had docked at one point at the port of the Land of Lightning. So maybe the Kumogakure ninja had gotten on the ship and gone somewhere with them?

But it was not going to be helpful if they had actually fled

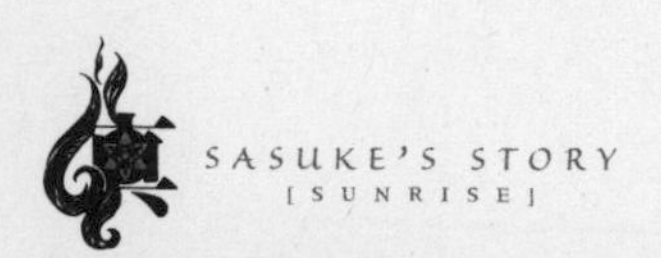

across the ocean. They wouldn't leave any footprints or scent; in the wide ocean, even the ninja dogs Kakashi could summon, all of them excellent trackers, would have a hard time finding the missing ninja. Kirigakure and Kumogakure were no doubt both at a loss for what to do.

If this were the past, the details of this incident would have stopped at the borders, but the letters seeking information had been sent to Konohagakure, Iwagakure, and Sunagakure—ninja villages of the five great lands—and now the information seemed to be spreading even further. Although this was another village's problem, it was not a stranger's problem.

When the information arrived, Kakashi conveyed it immediately to the ninja of Konoha. And to Sasuke, who was traveling the world. Kakashi suspected that genjutsu was involved. Although neither Kumogakure nor Kirigakure had any specific theories, they likely thought the same thing. And it had to be an unknown genjutsu. That was the only conclusion he could come to when he thought about the fact that so many ninja had been unable to grapple with it. Sasuke probably thought the same thing after reading Kakashi's letter.

Sasuke had left on his journey for information and atonement, saying something bothered him. Unlike the ninja in the village, he had some room to maneuver. And more than anything else, he had the sharingan and the rinnegan. Things other ninja couldn't know might be seen with his eyes.

"Sixth."

He heard a knock on the door of his office. Identifying the voice as that of Shizune, former Hokage Tsunade's student, he called out, "Yes, come in." She was kind enough to be his assistant as well.

The door was slightly ajar; Shizune poked her face through with a concerned expression. "Excuse me—Sai says he has a report," she informed him.

He had asked Sai to get in touch with Sasuke. So it was probably a report that his message had reached him.

Shizune looked worried, but Kakashi said, "Sure, show him in."

"All right, then." Shizune opened the door, and looked over her shoulder. "Excuse me."

"Hello!" Sai walked in with his usual somehow smarmy smile on his face. Behind him was Haruno Sakura, looking apologetic. A question mark popped up in Kakashi's mind.

Behind Sakura, one more person came into the room. "Hey! Master Kakashi!" Playing the fool with an unboundedly cheerful smile was the man who had saved the world in the last Great War, Uzumaki Naruto.

Sai was one thing. Why were Naruto and Sakura here?

"Of course it would be you, too."

Naruto clasped his hands behind his head and cackled. "Sai said he was coming to see you, so I just tagged along."

Without the slightest compunction.

"You too, Sakura?"

"I was looking something up with Shizune."

So when Sai and Naruto asked Shizune for a meeting with the Hokage, they had noticed Sakura there and invited her along, then.

"Anyway. How about I hear your report, Sai?"

"Right. My messenger safely reached Sasuke the other day."

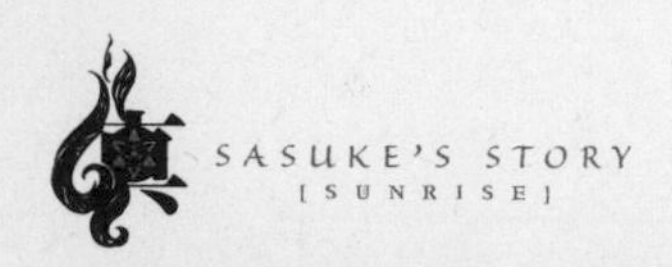

"The Cartoon Beast bird flew off to the northeast, hm? In which case, judging from the number of days, he's around Yugakure or Shimogakure, maybe?"

Hearing this, Sakura let out a sigh of relief. Sasuke was still alive somewhere. She felt easier, just knowing that.

"So, like, Master Kakashi, any progress in the disappearances?" Naruto unclasped the hands behind his head and looked at the letter in Kakashi's hands. He was clever at times.

"Apparently, there's no evidence or anything."

"Sixth, something's bothering us about this incident," Shizune said.

Sakura nodded and stepped forward. "It seems that we're seeing ninja missing from Konoha, as well."

"What?" Kakashi started to rise from his seated posture.

"It's not on the same large scale as in Kirigakure or Kumogakure, but there were several cases about three months ago. There might also be others that just weren't made public."

Even now, they had many dangerous missions, and sometimes, ninja did go missing. And because they had more frequent contact than before with other regions, there were more people coming and going. So this wasn't a special, rare occurrence—but something bothered Kakashi about it, too.

"Why were you looking into something like that, Sakura?"

Sakura was very busy as a medical ninja, and the fact that she was looking into something of this nature was a little unexpected. At his question, her gaze froze slightly.

"A regular at Ino's family's shop went on a trip and disappeared. Ino said he wasn't the sort of person to suddenly vanish, and when I heard about this case, I immediately remembered him."

Yamanaka Ino was a female ninja, Sakura's rival and best friend. Her family ran a flower shop, where Ino also worked from time to time. The sight of Ino worried about a regular customer had probably stuck in Sakura's mind.

"I thought I'd tell you once I learned more details."

Given that this was Sakura, there was no doubt she had been planning on telling him once she had looked into it enough to be sure.

"Oh, thanks. I'll keep an eye on it too."

Although the person on top was thought to have all the information, he actually didn't. For better or for worse, people sifted through information, deciding what was and wasn't worth telling the Hokage, so a lot of information never reached his ears. Which was why it was vital for him to hear the opinions of people he knew like this.

Good thing Sakura's story got to me at the right time, Kakashi thought as he turned his gaze to Naruto, who had brought Sakura in to begin with. It was at that moment...

"Sixth! There's an invader in the village!" A ninja from the barrier team appeared suddenly in the Hokage's office. Tension ran through the room.

"Did they touch the barrier?"

A spherical barrier had been set up around the village of Konohagakure, from the ground up into the sky. After the attack by Akatsuki, they had put up an even more powerful barrier.

"They...they're already inside the barrier, all the way to A-un gate..."

"What?!"

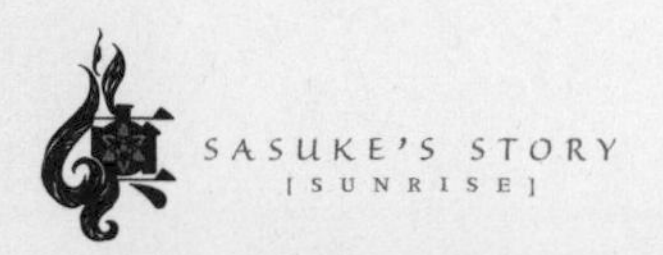

"The ninja of the barrier team are currently on their wa—" The end of the word didn't make it out.

Boom! They heard a sound like an explosion from somewhere. Kakashi and the others opened the windows of his office and looked outside.

"Master Kakashi, flames..." A fire had broken out in the direction Sakura was pointing, near the A-un gates, perhaps an effect of the explosion.

"Master Kakashi! We'll go check it out right now!" Naruto said.

Sai swiftly opened up a scroll hanging at his hip and sent his brush racing across it. The ink drew out a large bird with its wings spread. "Ninjutsu! Art of Cartoon Beast Mimicry!"

The bird flew up from the scroll as if being born and spread its large wings outside the window. Flapping them, the bird first allowed Sai to leap on; then, Naruto and Sakura followed suit.

"Do it," Kakashi said, tersely.

Naruto nodded, and the three flew off in the direction of the flames licking up into the air.

"Sixth, I'll go give the order for firefighting activities!" Shizune said, and Kakashi nodded in her direction before giving the order to gather information in all areas. He glanced at the letters from Kirigakure and Kumogakure laying on his desk.

"What exactly is going on here...?"

CHAPTER 1

∞

On the back of the enormous Cartoon Beast bird Sai had drawn, Naruto and the others hurried in the direction of the gates and the nearby fire. But when they were halfway there, Sai abruptly dropped their altitude and started flying low enough to scrape against the roofs of buildings.

"Sai, what's going on?!" Naruto shouted in surprise, when he spotted a three-person cell ahead of them racing along the rooftops toward A-un gate. "Oh! Shikamaru?!"

Sakura leaned forward and looked down. "Ino and Choji too! Sai, I can't believe you noticed them!"

The group of Ino-Shika-Cho had also apparently heard Naruto and Sakura.

"You guys're heading for A-un gate, too?" Shikamaru shouted, looking back.

"Get on!" Sai called out.

The three jumped up onto the enormous bird, and although the bird staggered and nearly crashed into a building the instant Choji was on board, Sai managed to get them flying high again immediately.

Naruto and the others looked once more at the three new arrivals. Shikamaru, Ino, and Choji were childhood friends, and they had previously joined together in a three-person cell under Sarutobi Asuma. However, now they each had their own positions, and didn't often work as a team anymore.

"Ino and her mother asked us to, so we've been chasing after traces of the regular customer from the flower shop," Shikamaru explained, reminding Naruto of Sakura's investigation

and what she had reported to Kakashi.

"You find any clues?" he asked.

"We found the inn that was probably the last place he stayed," Shikamaru replied. "The mistress there said he was on his way back to Konoha after a hot-spring treatment."

That meant that this customer hadn't planned to disappear.

"So then something happened on his way home," Naruto remarked.

Ino nodded firmly. "He—his name's Tadaichi, by the way. He lost his wife young. He's the sort of person who'd buy flowers at our shop and offer them to his wife whenever he had the time. He used to be active in the Anbu, but now he's fairly well on in years. He retired as a ninja this year, and when he came and said goodbye, he told us he was going to go around to the places where he spent time with his wife." He'd been a regular customer since Ino was little, so she was fond of him, unsurprisingly.

"Look. There's the whole thing with Kiri and Kumo right now, right? We're worried he got dragged into all that," Akimichi Choji interjected. "They're also investigating in Kumogakure, but it was raining at the time, so the scent got washed away. It's hard to find traces of him." Choji was in contact with Karui, a female ninja in Kumogakure, so he could get independent information.

"At any rate, before all of that, we need to do something about this situation," Shikamaru said, putting a stop to that conversation. He looked toward A-un gate. Within the gates, which were locked at night, flames licked up into the air inside of Konohagakure.

"Shikamaru, we were just at Master Kakashi's, and

apparently, there's an intruder in the village," Sakura told him. "Ninja from the barrier team are supposedly already on their way there."

"So then if we can spot the barrier team, we'll know the enemy?" Shikamaru said, and Naruto leaned far forward, straining his eyes.

"Over there!" Naruto's gaze was resting on the barrier team. They appeared to be fighting enemy ninja.

Shikamaru spotted them at the same time. He furrowed his brow. "What? They're totally on the defensive?"

Just as he noted, the ninja of the barrier team were retreating, almost as though they were trying to avoid actually fighting. Some were already injured, lying on the road.

"Huh?!" Ino suddenly cried out.

"What's wrong, Ino?" Sakura asked, but Ino didn't respond, instead moving to jump off by herself.

"Ino, that's dangerous." Sai grabbed her arm to stop her.

Ino's eyes were still on the enemy attacking the barrier team. "It can't be..."

"What's wrong, Ino?" Choji asked, seeing all the blood drain from her face.

Her lips trembled. "Tadaichi." She forced the name out.

"Huh?"

"It's Tadaichi!"

A shock ran through the group. The man Ino called Tadaichi was clad in travel gear, and the look on his face was blank, like it had been scraped off.

"You're sure, Ino?" Shikamaru asked.

"I'm totally sure! But he's not the kind of person to turn on

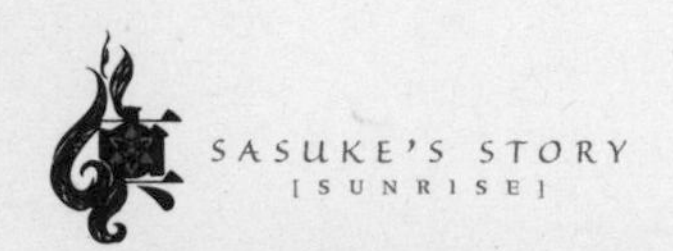

Konoha! Why..."

"So then..." Shikamaru looked down on Tadaichi. "Is there a possibility he's under a genjutsu...maybe?"

This time, Sakura gasped. She looked at the faces of the other enemies. "It might be exactly that, Shikamaru."

"What do you mean?"

The information she had just been reading on the missing people came back to life in her mind. "It's the people who went missing."

"What?!"

"They're Konoha ninja! They might all be!"

Shikamaru clicked his tongue and looked at the ninja of the barrier team. "So that's why they've been forced into a defensive battle!"

Someone on the barrier team had likely realized that the enemy warriors were Konoha ninja. But if it was genjutsu, then there was a chance they could be brought back to their senses with a counter-genjutsu. The barrier team was no doubt fighting with that very idea in mind. The attacks they threw at Tadaichi were too weak to kill.

"Wait, that," Naruto said. "What's that about?"

They felt a wave of pressure, like something swelling up and coming toward them.

Injured by the barrier team's attack, Tadaichi fell to the ground, and his body began shaking.

"Ah! This is bad!" Naruto immediately leapt off the bird.

Shadow Clones!! As he wove the signs in midair, his shadow clones landed next to the various members of the barrier team.

"Naruto?!"

"We're flying!" Without giving them a chance to say anything, Naruto lifted up the ninja of the barrier team, and all departed from the place at the same time.

When he looked back, Tadaichi was slowly getting to his feet. Despite the fact that he was injured, his face was still expressionless. The blood spilling out of his wounds frothed and bubbled. And that wasn't all. Lumps popped up all over his body, almost as if there were another living creature inside him, crawling around.

"We gotta get further back!" Naruto got more distance from Tadaichi before putting the barrier ninja down in what was probably a safe place, and then starting to run back to Tadaichi to try and help him.

But the lumps seething through Tadaichi's body swelled and grew larger, and his skin, unable to contain the growth, split. And then—

Boom!! He exploded violently like he was bursting open. The houses closest to him were unable to hold up against the impact of the explosion and were destroyed. Fortunately, Naruto's shadow clones had gone to check on and bring out the people in the buildings nearby, so there was no human damage, but new flames rose up into the sky.

"Are you okay, Naruto?!" Sakura cried, as Sai's Cartoon Mimicry bird landed and they all raced over to Naruto's side.

"Tadaichi..." Ino stared dumbfounded at the scene, bits of flesh flung everywhere. Sakura placed a concerned hand on her back. "I'm okay." She pulled herself together, and immediately ran over to the injured members of the barrier team with Sakura.

However, the threat had not ended.

"Hey, don't they seem kinda weird?" Shikamaru's face hardened as he stared at the ninja of Konoha, likely under someone's control. Until moments ago, they had been baring their teeth at the members of the barrier team, but now they suddenly turned their backs to them and started running. The Konoha ninja then spread out their hands on the wall that surrounded Konohagakure, and clung to it.

Naruto gasped. "No way! Them, too?!" He stared hard at their bodies. They were all injured somewhere—probably injuries from the explosion of Tadaichi. Blood oozed out of their wounds, and just like before, it was frothing. A chill ran up Naruto's spine. "Shikamaru! They're all gonna explode!"

"What?! If we have several explosions like that one at the same time, this whole area could be sent flying!"

There were nine Konoha ninja left. Their bodies began to transform and swell up, as if things inside were pushing outward.

Shikamaru clicked his tongue. "Can you make some wings with Art of Expansion?!" he yelled at Choji.

"G-got it!" Choji opened a bag of chips he had hidden on him, and shoved them all into his mouth. As he hurriedly chewed them up, he concentrated his power in his body. "Aaaaaaah!"

The secret technique of the Akimichi clan. In the blink of an eye, Choji's body became enormous, and butterfly wings sprouted on his back. This technique used a vast amount of chakra. Choji's cheeks, usually swollen, were carved out in sharp relief.

"How long 'till they explode, Naruto?!"

"Maybe ten seconds!"

Nine, eight, seven—

"Got it! Everyone, behind Choji! Hold onto something solid!"

Six, five, four—

"Choji, now! Flap those wings with everything you've got!"

"Aaah!" Having quickly grasped Shikamaru's intention, Choji braced himself and flapped the massive, chakra-made butterfly wings. He sent all of his own chakra out on the wind they created.

Three, two, one—

Booom! The noise of the explosion. And again and again. A series of these, and the bodies clinging to the wall were ripped apart all at once.

Shikamaru checked the front, and then yelled, "Here it comes!"

When the shock wave came toward the village of Konoha, it collided with the wind radiating outward from Choji's massive body. The wind hit the shock wave, and the two fought.

"I got your back!!" Naruto shouted. "Here we go, Kurama!"

Right!

To reinforce Choji's wind, Naruto called up the nine-tailed Kurama, once a source of hatred, now his partner. Power raced through his body, generating a Wind Release: Ransengan that he sent flying toward the shock wave. This new wind pushed back the shock wave to protect the village.

"All right. Nice!"

After wrestling with Choji's wind, the shock wave was bounced back beyond the village with the added force of Naruto's Wind Release: Ransengan. The trees of the forest just outside the gates were whipped around by the combination of wind

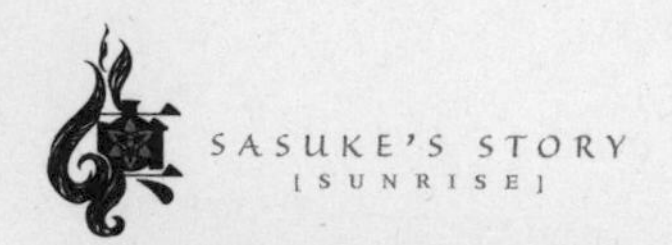

and shock wave and flattened.

"Hah, hah...Did that. Do. The trick?" Choji released his jutsu, breathing hard.

Part of the wall enclosing Konoha was destroyed, but there appeared to be no damage to the village. The flames rising up inside the village had also been blown out.

Shikamaru patted Choji's shoulder. "Nice work."

Sakura raced over to the broken wall, but her shoulders dropped with regret. The bodies had been turned into hunks of flesh beyond repair. Ino also bit her lip.

"At any rate, we gotta report to the Hokage. Sai, sorry, can you take us with your Cartoon Mimicry?" Shikamaru quickly gave instructions. Naruto also moved to follow Shikamaru.

"Naruto!"

Just as Sai pulled out his brush, they heard someone suddenly call out Naruto's name. They looked in that direction and saw a man with wide-framed sunglasses and spiky black hair swept up and back running over to the scene.

"Huh? Who're you again?" The man looked familiar, but his name wouldn't come out.

"Yamashiro Aoba!"

"Yamashiro Aoba?"

"We went to Turtle Island in Kumogakure together!"

"Ohh! Yeah, right! Huh? What? You going to Turtle Island again?"

"Not that! I'm a messenger from the Hokage!" Aoba shouted out the main point, sensing a danger that the conversation would continue to go in this strange circle.

"From Master Kakashi? What's he say?"

"Earlier, intruders were detected by the barrier. They number thirty."

"What?!" they all cried out in surprise. Thirty—three times the attack just now.

"Does that mean new intruders?" Sakura asked. "They were detected this time?"

"Yes." Aoba nodded. "They're heading this way now."

Naruto felt eyes on him from the woods on the other side of the destroyed wall. "There!"

From the dark woods, first, a lone man. He was followed by one more, and then another.

"That may be..." Sakura murmured, a bewildered look on her face.

They were wearing ninja uniforms. But they were a mix of Kirigakure and Kumogakure uniforms. The marks of those two villages were also carved into their forehead protectors.

"This looks like it's gonna be a drag," quick-thinking Shikamaru grumbled. "Naruto, you guys were with the Sixth—Master Kakashi, right? You heard that someone had invaded the village, and you came running to the scene. From all this so far, I'm guessing that the barrier team didn't notice the first intruders until they were in the village."

"Y-yeah."

Shikamaru talked as though he had actually been there himself. "Although they were being controlled by someone, Tadaichi and the others were Konoha ninja. That's why they were able to slip through the barrier without being noticed. They were probably just a teaser, at best."

The army corps of mind-controlled ninja was slowly

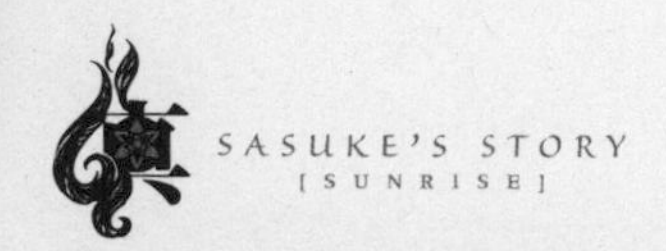

approaching. Dull eyes that gave no impression of will. This was the main force.

"On top of that, there's a good chance that these guys here now are the missing ninja from Kiri and Kumo. Honestly, it's just one thing after another." Shikamaru scratched his head.

"Shikamaru—the trigger that makes them explode is probably getting hurt. Their wounds emit a strange chakra and starts the transformation of their bodies." Just like Naruto had noticed their wounds, Sakura had also apparently picked out the trigger for the explosions.

"In which case, we can't be careless with them." A serious look rose up on Shikamaru's face as he stared at the approaching ninja.

And this situation was not just happening in Konoha.

∞

"Why would the ninja from the alliance training corps be here?"

Unlike Konoha, where few of its own ninja had shown up, Kirigakure had had several dozen of their own thrown at them right from the start, and these ninja had made it into the interior of the village. Fighting to defend Kiri's key facilities, Chojuro gritted his teeth at the smoke rising up in every direction.

"Chojuro, the evacuation of the elderly and the children is complete," The Mizukage appeared before him to report the end of the evacuation. "I'm going." She started to run off to the central area of the battle. "Tell them to follow me. I have a duty to protect the people of the village. That...means them too." She looked at the smoke wafting up in tufts, unlike the fog that always hung over the village. These mind-controlled people were also ninja of Kirigakure.

"I'll protect you, Lady Mizukage—the village of Kirigakure...absolutely!"

"Mm, I'm counting on you."

∞

"Boss! Please leave this to us! Sorry!"

"Ngh!"

Similarly, the ninja of Kumogakure also stared at their completely changed comrades. The Raikage was itching to join in the fight, but Darui, the Raikage's right hand, saw that there was a risk of causing more damage if he did, so he was holding the village chief back.

"Shouldn't we be calling Killer B?!" Omoi brought up his mentor Killer B, imagining the worst-case scenario.

"There'll be too much chaos!" all the ninja around him shouted.

"C, haven't you detected the true identity of the enemy yet?!" Darui turned his gaze on the sensor ninja C.

C frowned and shook his head from side to side.

∞

Their opponents were ninja under a genjutsu. And if you hurt them, they exploded. They had no will of their own. What on earth were they supposed to do?

"Naruto!"

A new voice rang out. He turned around and saw a woman running toward him, long hair swinging.

"Hinata?!"

"After you noticed Tadaichi's explosion and jumped back, I called her through Ino," Shikamaru said to the stunned Naruto.

Born into the main family of the Hyuga clan, Hinata was the possessor of the byakugan. She had a wide field of vision and the ability to see through things, among others.

"Hinata, it seems like everyone's under a genjutsu. Is there someone controlling them somewhere?"

"Understood. I'll look." Hinata—now also Naruto's wife—focused her power in her eyes. The blood vessels popped up one after another and then her eyes opened.

Byakugan!

She examined the area with the visual power to see through everything. She stretched her mind out into the woods and the surrounding buildings, not letting a single thing get away from her.

"So?"

"It seems like there's no one."

"What? There's no one?!" Sakura shouted in surprise. "Then how were they being controlled?"

"But there's foreign chakra running through the bodies of those people."

"What d'you mean, Hinata?"

Hinata's byakugan had seen it, foreign chakra running through every inch of their bodies. Such a slight aura that it couldn't be seen without the byakugan. It was possible that this was what was controlling them.

"So then, we just have to take out that chakra!" If they just got rid of the source, the problem would be resolved. That's what Naruto thought, but Hinata's face remained clouded.

"That chakra...it's moving around like part of the body. It might have fused within their bodies."

And on top of that, they would have to get rid of the chakra without causing external injuries.

"So we're not going to be able to just tear it out." Shikamaru sighed. "How about we start with capturing them without actually hurting them?"

Ino furrowed her brow. "But, Shikamaru, it's going to be tough to capture that many people without hurting them. And they're sticking together like dumplings."

Just as Ino noted, the ninja approaching Konoha were moving in a tight group. If one of them got injured and exploded, it would set off the others, and they would all go up in flames.

"Ah!" Naruto jerked his head up. The eyes of the entire group turned toward him. "I just got a great idea!"

"I see. It's simple, but it'll probably work." Shikamaru grinned after hearing Naruto out.

Naruto grinned back and then looked at Hinata. "It works for you too, right, Hinata?"

Hinata nodded firmly. "Yeah."

"So then, let's do this!" Naruto took the lead. He kicked at the ground and started running. As he ran, he activated his Shadow Clone technique and moved forward in a V with his real self at the apex. The mind-controlled ninja caught sight of him, and recognized him as an enemy.

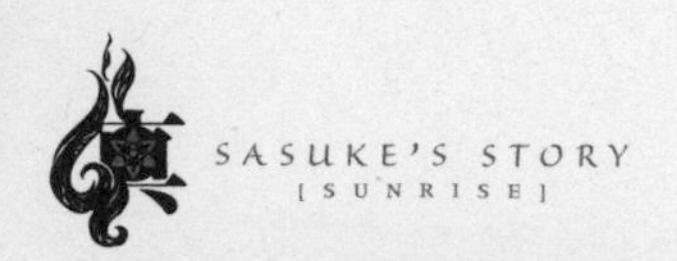

In that instant, the Narutos ran off in all directions like baby spiders.

"Hey! Over here!"

"No, no! Over here!"

"I'm here! Come on! See!"

He was deliberately provoking them. It wasn't clear whether it worked or not, but the ninja scattered and began to chase after Naruto's clones. He opened up the distance between the enemies.

"Okay. Here we go!" Shikamaru turned his eyes on one of the mind-controlled ninja who was far enough out that there wouldn't likely be other damage whatever happened, brought his hands together, and wove signs.

Shadow Possession!

His shadow, lit up by the gentle light of the moon, stretched out toward his opponent.

"Okay!" His shadow connected with his opponent's, and the man suddenly stopped on the spot. Shikamaru spread his legs slightly and dropped his arms to his sides, and his opponent did the same thing. "Hinata!"

"Yes!" With the byakugan, Hinata looked at the man's pressure points. The one she was aiming for was a quick cut-off pressure point. She stretched out an index finger. She absolutely could not miss. She imagined the movements of Hyuga Neji, the greatest genius since the start of the Hyuga clan.

"Hah!" Her finger shot out in alignment with her breathing and dug into the man's body. After the span of a breath, the strength slipped out of him. She had stabbed the cutoff pressure point correctly.

Shikamaru released his Shadow Possession and the man's body listed to one side.

"You did it!" Having led the man away, Naruto's shadow clone now held him up as he looked at Hinata.

"With the pressure point activated, he shouldn't be able to move for a day." Just as Hinata noted, the man was limp in Naruto's arms.

If they used this method, they could completely stop their enemies. But it required a great deal of concentration, thus placing a serious burden on Hinata.

"You okay, Hinata?" Naruto asked, with concern.

"I'm okay," she replied. "We're fighting together."

Naruto nodded sharply.

As if this was his signal, Shikamaru said, "Okay then, let's take them all down." This time, Shikamaru's shadow reached out to all the mind-controlled ninja.

A simple task repeated. But thanks to this, all the ninja were safely secured, and now lay quietly on the ground. It seemed that the issue was resolved, but the faces of Naruto and his friends were still dark.

"It won't work." Trying to release the genjutsu, Sakura attempted a counter-genjutsu, but there was no change in the foreign chakra racing through their bodies. "After a while, the effect of the pressure point's going to end. If this looks like it's going to drag on, we'll have to hit the cutoff pressure point again, before they regain consciousness."

"Dang, so we can't take our eyes off them. It would be great if they at least knew what was going on," Shikamaru remarked.

Aoba, who had come with a message from Kakashi, reached

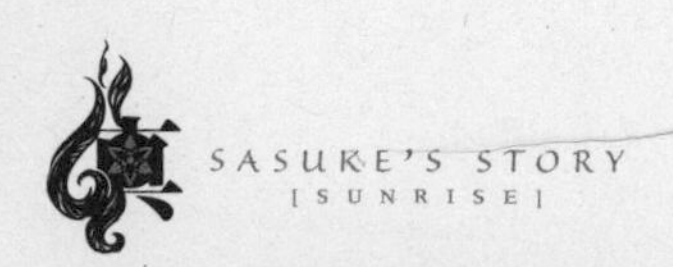

out his hands. "Maybe I'll just try." He was going to look into their memories.

"Will you be okay?" Naruto asked.

Aoba glanced at him. "I'm not as good as Inoichi, but I'll give it a try."

Inoichi was Ino's father. He gave up his life in the Fourth Great Ninja War. His sensing had been excellent even among the Yamanaka clan, and he had been active in the role of connecting ninja.

Aoba placed his left hand on the forehead of a Kirigakure ninja, and his right hand on his own forehead. "Okay, I'm going in." He linked his opponent's consciousness with his own and flew into the world of memory.

Normally, Aoba would be able to see into his opponent's brain like this. "Ngh! This—!" But the instant he went into the other mind, his field of view was dyed completely red. Narrowing his eyes, he saw a red sea spreading out at his feet. The lapping ripples reacted to the intruder, and turned into enormous waves.

"Damn. A genjutsu trap?! I've never seen this kind of offensive genjutsu trap before." He immediately tried to run away, but the waves swept his body away, and pulled him into a vortex of thought.

"Hey, Sakura, doesn't he seem kinda weird?" Naruto asked, sensing a turbulent aura as he watched over Aoba. Aoba's mouth was half open and he swayed back and forth, as if rocked by waves.

"There was a genjutsu trap in his mind!" Sakura shouted.

"That's bad, isn't it?!" Ino's face stiffened, but she quickly brought her fingertips together as if she had resolved herself, and set her sights on Aoba.

Mind Transmission Jutsu!

The secret Mind Transmission technique of the Yamanaka clan. Ino entered Aoba's consciousness, and her body slumped over. Reacting instantly, Shikamaru held her up with his Shadow Possession.

"Are you okay, Ino?!" Sakura's eyes shot back and forth between Ino and Aoba.

The contest was an instant, but for Ino and Aoba, it must have been much longer.

"Haah!" Aoba took a deep breath and dropped to his knees. "Sorry. Thanks." Perhaps he had exerted himself too much mentally; Aoba put both hands on the ground and breathed deeply, his shoulders heaving.

"We sorted it out." Ino's face was pale after releasing the Mind Transmission jutsu.

"Ino!"

"You know that time when I went into you, and there was another you getting in my way? Aoba fought like that." Ino smiled at Sakura, her face drained of all blood. But that was as far as her show of courage went.

"Ino!"

Having lost a great deal of chakra, Ino passed out. Aoba also collapsed.

"Sai! Take Ino and Aoba to the hospital! I'll take a look at them!" Sakura shouted. She had been trained in the medical ninja arts directly under the former Hokage, Tsunade, and she sent chakra into Ino and Aoba.

Sai quickly set his brush moving.

In the midst of all this, paying no mind to the commotion, the sun began to climb into the eastern sky. Under its light, sweat spilled down Naruto's cheeks.

Naruto had secretly picked up on it. The bottomless hatred planted inside of them.

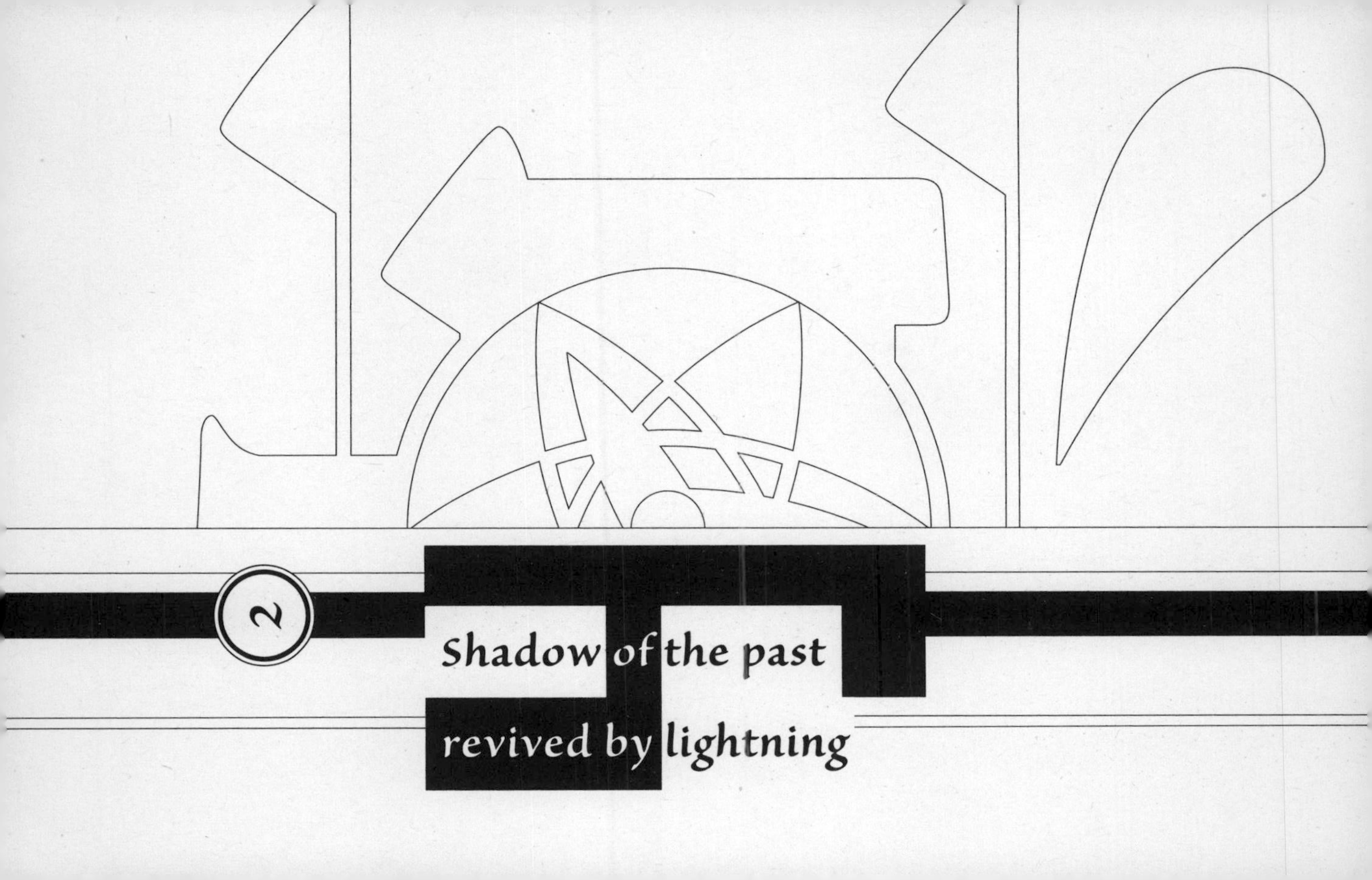
2
Shadow of the past
revived by lightning

CHAPTER 2

Shadow of the past revived by lightning

1

"Oh, you know, now that I think about it, do you actually need us?" Chino muttered, an annoyed look on her face, as she slipped through the bamboo grove and the forest spread out around her. "The whole thing could be taken care of if we just left it all to Sassy."

When the sun rose, Iou had appeared and shouted, "All of you, hurry up and find Dark Thunder and defeat them, already!"

Sasuke had planned to go out and search on his own, but then this obstacle had popped up. So in the end, he was heading toward the village where Iou's daughter had died, together with Chino and Nowaki.

"I can go by myself," Sasuke said.

The grumbling Chino pursed her lips. "When you basically come right out and say you don't need us, I actually want to fight back, though!"

He didn't recall going that far, but it was indeed as she said.

"We'll give it our all!" she shouted, looking angry. "You're not going to beat us, Sassy!"

"I don't care. Stop calling me that, though."

"The fact that you're saying that means that you totally do care! And I'm older than you, Sassy, so I can give you a nick-name!"

At first glance, Chino appeared, from any angle, to be a girl of around ten, but she was apparently older than he was. He could sense the wealth of her knowledge and experience, so she probably wasn't lying, but he wasn't quite satisfied with the idea, somehow.

You shouldn't judge people by appearances or preconceptions. The words popped up in the back of his mind. They were his brother, Itachi's. He had heard them when he was very little.

At the time, Uchiha Shisui, someone Itachi was very close with, had been pessimistic about the future of the Uchihas and had thrown himself in the Nakano River. The people of the Uchiha clan suspected that Itachi had killed him. Itachi had raised a hand against these people. They had been convinced Itachi would never lay a hand on them no matter what they said, and Itachi told them that they shouldn't judge people based on appearances or preconceptions alone.

When Sasuke thought about it now, Itachi had probably been furious and sad at the time. Without even attempting to learn the first thing about Shisui's feelings, after the young man had given his life for the sake of the Uchiha clan, they interpreted the situation to suit their own cause and turned it into a means of attacking someone else. The Uchiha karma.

The third Hokage, Hiruzen, had said that from the time he was little, Itachi was a sensitive child, who had noticed the signs and teachings of his predecessors that no one else paid heed to and picked up on the goings-on of other ninja and the village

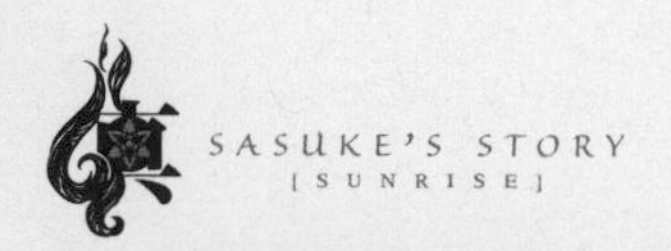

without anyone telling him. Rather than being a slave to the bonds of the clan, he was able to think of what lay ahead for the ninja, for the village; he considered the future and worried about it.

Are you going to join too?

He had once asked Itachi about the path he was proceeding down. The place was in front of the Konoha Police headquarters. The police force, founded by Uchiha ancestors, was a division in charge of ninja crime that contributed to maintaining the peace in the village. Their father Fugaku worked as the chief there, so Sasuke asked if Itachi would also go to work there.

Dunno, we'll have to see... Itachi's response was vague.

Having no idea at the time that the police was an organization to corral the Uchiha clan, or about the talk of Itachi joining the Anbu, Sasuke had innocently said, *Do it! When I grow up...I'm gonna join the police force too!!*

This was the dream of a foolish little brother who knew precisely nothing. But Itachi had simply answered, *Yeah.*

His field of view had been far-reaching and broad; he was a presence that went beyond the framework of Konoha. Still, perhaps he had responded that way because he too dreamed of the two brothers on the police force together, tackling their daily duties alongside each other.

Sasuke still had complicated feelings about the fact that this Itachi had been sacrificed for the Uchiha clan, for Konoha. There had been a time when he thought of nothing but restoring Itachi's honor. But Itachi wouldn't have wanted that.

Brought back to life by Edotensei, Itachi had placed his hand on the back of Sasuke's head when they parted, pulled their foreheads together, looked straight into Sasuke's eyes and spoken. *I will love you always.*

Because what Itachi wanted to leave to this world in the end wasn't resentment or hatred toward it, but rather his feelings of love for his little brother. He could've cared less about restoring his honor. But apparently, Naruto was telling people that after he was brought back with the Edotensei, Itachi had helped them for the sake of the world. Naruto would have known about the coup d'état, but without touching on that, he simply offered up Itachi's name as one of the ninja who had helped him out in the Great War.

Sasuke didn't expect that this would make everyone simply accept it, but there was no one who doubted Naruto. Even if there had been, Naruto would no doubt have not given up, but simply continued to tell his story. Putting aside the question of whether Itachi would have wanted it, perhaps the day would come when the feeling that Itachi had some kind of reason for what he did would sprout in Konoha.

"That reminds me. So, like, Sassy, are you heading home to Konohagakure?" Chino asked him, perhaps bored with traveling.

Given that he had just been thinking about Konoha, his heart skipped a beat, but he said nothing.

"Oh! So you're ignoring me?! Don't you need to rebuild the Uchihas or something? I mean, there's only the one still alive."

He remained silent.

"Hellooooo! Hellooooo! Can you hear me?!"

"Chino, quit it," Nowaki finally chided Chino, after holding his tongue until that point.

"Whose side are you on?!" Her shouts made his eardrums

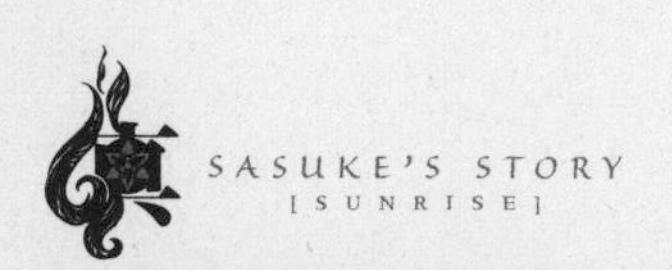

vibrate, and Sasuke quietly dropped his gaze.

For him, the village of Konohagakure was a vortex of love and hate. But perhaps the time had come when he had to come up with an answer to the question of how to deal with it.

∞

About three hours from Takeno was the village where Iou's daughter had lived.

"Just awful..." Chino murmured, unconsciously, upon seeing the state of the village.

The houses had been destroyed, and on the walls that were left, traces of discolored blood remained. When they entered a house through a large hole, they saw the inside was also in complete disarray. Everything of monetary value had been taken.

At Sasuke's feet, a stuffed animal stiffened with blood lay on its side. Framed pictures had fallen onto the floor, and in one of them, a small girl clutched this very stuffed animal, grinning alongside her family.

"Didn't the nearby ninja villages respond?" Sasuke asked.

"It seems that Yugakure is moving, but the level of the ninja there isn't actually the greatest." Nowaki sighed. "The other village that's close is Shimogakure, but they're not touching this case. Even if the villagers did set out to ask the land for a mission, it'd be a dangerous road, given they can barely use any ninja arts. To begin with, the villagers of this area are so scared of the Dark Thunder group now that they hesitate to even step out of their villages."

"That's why they've got no choice but to grab onto travelers like us who happen to pass through," Chino added.

They meet such a terrible fate as this and yet there's no helping hand? Sasuke felt like he was being shown a clear picture of the absurdity of the world.

"Konoha's huge, so you're guaranteed the basics, I guess, but most places are like this. Absurd," Chino said, as she looked up at the traces of blood on the ceiling. "If we're talking well known, maybe Amegakure? That place is surrounded by the Land of Fire, the Land of Wind, and the Land of Earth, so every time the great nations went to war, it got dragged into it. No matter what the era or which country, it's kids who get the short end of the stick." Chino picked up the stuffed animal and the photo, and set them together on the shelf.

Unless they caught the Dark Thunder group as soon as possible, a similar tragedy would likely unfold once more. He had to get information on them. "'You fallen Dark Thunder.'"

"Hm?"

"That's what Iou said yesterday. What did he mean by 'fallen'?" Sasuke remembered what the old man had said because that part bothered him, somehow.

"Ohh, the Dark Thunder group, I guess they used to work as sort of gentlemen thieves."

"Gentlemen thieves?"

"Yeah. They'd hit bad guys, take their money, and then give it to the poor. Although back then, they were called the Bright Lightning Group."

"I guess it's only since they changed their name to Dark Thunder that they've been pushing the limits of cruelty," Nowaki added.

So then they were originally an ally of the weak? It was hard to understand why they would flip to the exact opposite position—but Sasuke knew it only took an instant to fall into darkness. No matter what you might live through, a single incident could turn the world upside down. Love into hate, kindness into curses, bonds into isolation.

The Uchihas had been a deeply loving clan. Thus, when they lost that love, sometimes, everything was painted over and transformed into hate. It had been the second Hokage, Senju Tobirama, who said that. Having been isolated and made to grow up with the power of hatred, Sasuke's way of life had maybe proven Tobirama right. Although he had come through out of the darkness, he contained the latent potential for something similar to happen in the future. A violent impulse that ate into reason slept within his body.

In order to not commit the same error again, Sasuke needed to be alone, and have the time to reexamine himself. He would likely never in his whole life put it into words, but he couldn't betray the trust of his friends. No, he didn't want to betray it. Which was exactly why he had to learn how to control this Uchiha blood. Because if he made connections, then he would inevitably have to experience parting, and losing that love at some point. Naruto had said he would stop him if he took the wrong path again, but next time, he wanted to stand on his own two feet.

That reminds me. So, like, Sassy, are you heading home to Konohagakure?

He had several reasons for not returning to the village, but there was likely also a part of him that was afraid of making intimate connections with other people.

"Hey? What're we going to do now? You wanna look around here a little more?"

Sasuke looked around the ruined village again. From Iou's story, he could guess that they also had no mercy on women and children, but this was really too awful a torment for weak opponents who couldn't really fight back. It made him want to ask if they had some serious grudge against this village.

Iou had probably seen the body of his dead daughter here, after she had been cruelly ripped apart. It was perhaps no wonder he sought revenge.

While he thought about this, Chino suddenly sat down on the spot. She put her ear to the ground and closed her eyes.

"What's the matter?"

"I felt like it moved just now."

"Moved?"

"The water underground." Ear still pressed to the earth, Chino wove signs. Nowaki put his index finger to his lips to indicate that Sasuke should be quiet. Chino's body was enveloped in chakra, and this began to enter the earth. "I'm connected. It *is* moving... Something's closing in on Takeno."

So was she a sensor ninja?

Karin, a member of Taka, was also excellent at sensing; she could see through to the nature of, and changes in, chakra that even Sasuke couldn't even begin to understand. It wasn't a surprise to find a sensor like Chino, who could feel things over long distances.

"Dark Thunder?"

"It could be." As she stood up, Chino looked up at Sasuke.

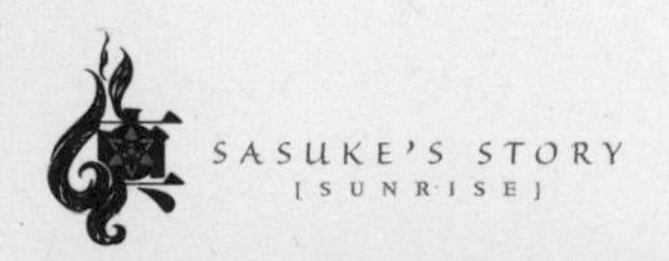

"We're going back." Sasuke kicked at the ground, and charged through the village into the woods. He leapt over the tree roots and jumped from branch to branch, gradually gaining speed. Chino and Nowaki chased after him frantically.

It had taken them three hours to get from Takeno to Iou's daughter's village, but Sasuke had taken his time with that trip, searching out the surrounding areas for any auras or other clues. Now he was practically running in a mad dash, and he quickly closed the distance to Takeno.

When the trees finally start to open up into the bamboo grove, they heard the loud *boom* of an explosion.

"Sassy, I smell smoke!"

Takeno was upwind. When they saw it, there was no doubt what was happening. Sasuke ran even faster, the bamboo leaves crunching under his feet.

"Aaah! Heeeelp!"

He heard the sharp cry of a woman. When he looked in that direction, he saw a young woman fleeing from the direction of the village toward them. Behind her, men with leering grins on their faces chased after her. Nowaki shouted.

"Sasuke, it's the Dark Thunder group!"

The men held swords in their hands and brandished them at the woman.

"Ha ha! We're killing everyone!"

"Aaaaah!" In a single fluid movement, Sasuke pulled a kunai from his pocket and threw it.

"Aaoh?!" The kunai knocked away the sword aiming for the woman's neck just as it was on the verge of striking. "Wh-who are you...?"

The enemy were three in number. Without replying to their question, he pulled out three more kunai, and released them in the direction of the woman.

"Eeep!"

"Hey! You're gonna hit—" Chino raised a voice in panic, but all the kunai slipped past the woman and plunged into the bodies of the men behind her.

"Ngaaah!"

Sasuke leapt over the woman's head and landed right next to one of the men felled by his kunai, lying face up on the ground. Sasuke closed his eyes, focused his power there, and then opened them again. His red sharingan with the three *tomoe* marks. He caught the man's gaze with these eyes.

"Ee. Kah...hah..."

Control via genjutsu. Foam spilled out of the man's mouth. He wouldn't be able to move for a while.

"It's Sasuke. It's Sasuke of the sharingan! We have to tell Lord Karyu—" the second man yelled, yanking the kunai out of his body and getting to his feet.

Sasuke somersaulted across the bamboo leaves, leaned in toward the man's feet, pressed his right hand to the ground, and pushed his lower body up. The sole of his left foot kicked out, and caught the man on the chin. The blow gave the man a concussion, and his eyes rolled back to the whites as he dropped to the ground. And that was two.

"Ee, eep..." The last man gave a pathetic cry and tried to run. Sasuke unsheathed his sword and let his chakra flow into it. With the blade enveloped in crackling electricity, he thrust it at the man's defenseless back.

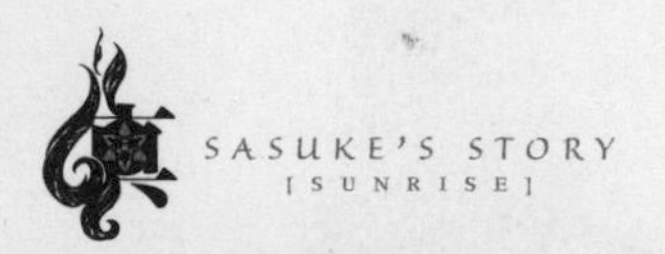

"Gah gah gah gah gah gah gah gah gah gah gah!" The electricity poured into the man's body, and he collapsed from the shock. With that, all three of the men who had been chasing the woman were on the ground.

"...Scary!"

"Instant kill—"

"I didn't kill them." Sasuke shook off the electricity and sheathed his sword before surveying the area. It appeared other villagers were fleeing as well, and being chased by the Dark Thunder group. He moved to help them, but then, he heard another loud explosion from the village.

"Sassy! We'll deal with the escaping villagers somehow. You go to the village!" Chino had apparently also sensed the enemies; she ran off in that direction. Nowaki pulled out a chakra blade and followed her.

Deciding to leave them to handle that situation, Sasuke ran toward the village. When he slipped through the bamboo, he found the villagers sitting on the ground, motionless. It seemed that their legs had been injured and they couldn't move. So Dark Thunder was planning to torture and kill them, once they ensured the villagers couldn't get away.

"Him?"

In the center of the village, a man stood, holding a ball in each hand. He appeared to be the leader.

"You! Karyu! So you finally showed yourself in this village!" Iou stood in front of this Karyu. He was already hurt in various places; blood dripped down from his forehead. All he had was his bamboo lance. But he gripped it tightly and charged at Karyu.

"As if that's going to work!" Karyu threw one of the balls at

Iou. The instant it hit Iou in the stomach, it bounced back with a *crack*. Iou went flying and slammed into the wall of his house behind him.

"Ngah!" An enormous amount of blood jetted out of his mouth.

"Now then, let's go for the head, shall we?" Karyu took aim at the head of Iou—slumped down, back against the wall—and threw the other ball to strike the final blow. Iou couldn't move a muscle.

The fierce sound of the house being destroyed echoed through the village, and once the dust settled, there was a gaping hole in the wall.

"Hmm?"

But Iou was nowhere to be seen.

"B-brat..."

Seconds before, Sasuke had grabbed onto Iou's clothes and yanked him away.

"Hm, oh, ohhhhhh?" Karyu looked at Sasuke and blinked several times, before a look of delight rose up onto his face. "I never dreamed I'd actually get to meet you, Sasuke...!" He appeared thrilled to the bone. "Uchiha Sasuke! I've admired you so much! The man who burned with revenge for his clan, and stuck to his own principles, even going so far as to take on the world! I've wanted to meet you! I've wanted so much to meet you!"

Just as Nowaki had said, Karyu adored Sasuke. The Sasuke from when he was steeped in darkness. Karyu spread both arms wide as if to show his appreciation.

In contrast, Sasuke looked at Karyu with a feeling of disgust.

"What, boy? You're with Karyu?!" Holding back the blood

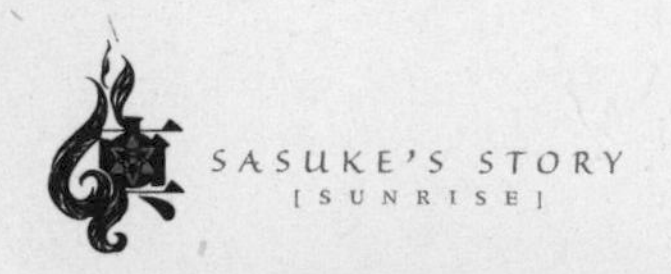

oozing out of his side, Iou suddenly turned suspicious eyes on Sasuke. Apparently, he had already forgotten that Sasuke had saved him.

"Ha! You really are a self-serving old man," Karyu murmured, exasperated. It seemed they knew each other.

"Sh-shut up! Enough outta you, you evil man! Anything's fine, boy! He killed my daughter! He's the root of all evil! Hurry up and kill this man!"

"What're you talking about, old man? Sasuke's my hero, you know." Karyu's eyes glittered. "So obviously, it'll be me killing Sasuke!" He brought his hands together. "I will go beyond you!!"

Hardly listening to Karyu's proclamations, Sasuke clad his unsheathed blade in electricity and aimed the tip at the other man's stomach.

"Whoops! Can't let you do that!"

Earth Style! Mud Wall!

A wall of earth shot up with great force from within the ground. Karyu continued to weave signs.

Lava Style! Rubber Wall!

Karyu bent his torso back, and expelled what rose up from within his body at the wall.

Sasuke's sword touched the wall, and the electric charge vanished.

"Rubber is resistant to Lightning Style!"

A wall of earth enveloped in rubber. It appeared that Karyu had a kekkei genkai called Lava Style that produced rubber. Hidden behind this wall, Karyu continued to knead his chakra. "Your boss is serious this time. Everyone, get back!"

The men of Dark Thunder flew out of the village like they were running away.

Lava Style! Rubber Ball!

Karyu called out the technique name, and balls of various sizes shot out of his mouth, rolling along the ground. The rolling spheres looked like traditional woven Japanese balls.

"Gah ha! And now!" Karyu slowly raised his arms. As he did, the balls bobbed up into the air. Conversely, when he lowered his hands, the balls dropped. In line with his hand movements, the balls began to bounce somewhat eerily. "Here we go!"

Karyu punched a ball close to him with his fist. He whirled his body around and hit a different ball with a backhand blow. He kicked a ball flying low to the ground in front of him before grabbing the final ball to his side, leaping up high, and flinging it at Sasuke. The four balls closed in on Sasuke, each with its own trajectory.

However, it wasn't difficult to read those trajectories. Sasuke dodged the balls and tried to get closer to Karyu.

"We're just beginning!" Karyu sensed Sasuke's movements, and wove signs.

A protrusion suddenly rose up beneath Sasuke's feet. The ground continued to rise. When he was about to lose his balance, a new ball came flying at him. Sasuke flipped backward, and twisted around to dodge it.

"Still more to come!" Karyu used Earth Style and created high walls, one after another. As he did, the balls he had released hit them and bounced back, creating even more complicated trajectories.

The balls closed in on Sasuke from all directions.

"Tch!"

One of them hit his thigh. The ball bounced lightly back, but it had no sooner hit him than a dull pain ran through the bone like an echo. The balls likely contained kneaded chakra to increase the power of a hit. He would get nowhere like this. Sasuke tried to catch Karyu in a genjutsu with his sharingan.

"C'mon, then! Try and catch me!" Karyu grabbed a villager whose legs had been broken so he couldn't run away, and thrust him forward.

"Eee, eee! Stoooooop!" the villager screamed, pushed forward like a shield.

Sasuke shifted his gaze momentarily. "Tch!"

Karyu didn't just say he adored Sasuke; he had actually looked into Sasuke in some detail.

When Sasuke tried to get closer, the balls got in his way, and if he used any big techniques, the villagers would be dragged into it. Or rather, the entire village might be destroyed. The techniques he could use to stop Karyu with minimal damage were limited.

"You...you monster...!" Iou shouted.

At Iou's unthinking cry, Karyu laughed, still clutching the villager. "A monster has no right to call me a monster!"

"What did you say?!"

Karyu flung the villager down to the ground and glared at Iou. Although he had seemed to be having great fun up to that point, he turned serious for a moment. "The second things aren't convenient for you, you toss us aside. How do you have any right to say anything to anyone?"

"Ngh, hngh..."

Sasuke hadn't heard anything about this from Iou. But what was important to him at that moment was not their stories. The bouncing balls. The Earth Style walls that appeared when he tried to get closer. The Lava Style rubber that snuffed out electricity. And the people being held hostage.

Sasuke's eyes, his sharingan, memorized the state of this hectic movement. And then finally, they reflected Iou and the bamboo grove. Sasuke turned his back to Karyu.

"Hm? Hey!" Karyu shouted. "Where are you going?!"

Sasuke ignored him, and stepped into Iou's house through the ruined wall.

"...This." Just as he grabbed ahold of the object he wanted, an enormous ball assaulted Iou's house. Immediately escaping the building, Sasuke poured his chakra into the object he had acquired.

"Hah!" Jumping up high with the rising earthen wall as a foothold, Sasuke aimed for Karyu.

"Ha ha! I have these rubber walls!" Karyu moved to protect himself with the rubber walls as he had done throughout the fight.

However, the rubber bounced back, and the earthen wall that appeared beneath it crumbled. Not only that—the balls all around Karyu were all destroyed at once.

"Wh-what's going on?! I don't know this technique!" Karyu dropped his surprised gaze to his feet, and saw a bamboo skewer stuck there. One of the ones Iou had made. "A skewer?! You couldn't possibly have kneaded your chakra into a skewer and destroyed the rubber?!"

The tapered point of the bamboo. And this was just a diversion.

"Dammit!" At the moment Karyu sensed the aura and gasped, he heard the call of a plover signaling the end.

∞

Once Sasuke had defeated Karyu and taken care of the members of the Dark Thunder group who had been watching things play out from outside the village, Chino and Nowaki brought the villagers back. They were all injured in some way or another, but fortunately, none of them had been killed. The men of the Dark Thunder group were restrained inside of the shed in the village for the time being.

"Sassy, looks like they're waking up."

Evening fell, and when Karyu regained consciousness, Sasuke and the others went into the shed.

"Ha ha! Quite the sorry state, hm?" Karyu murmured, looking at himself and his comrades tied up around him. Then he looked up at Sasuke, before shifting his gaze to Iou. At the sight of Iou with bandages wound around his stomach, Karyu let out a contemptuous laugh.

Iou flushed red with anger at this challenge. "I thought I told you to kill him! So why is he locked up in here?!" Iou complained to Sasuke.

Sasuke looked down on Karyu. "You said you were tossed aside. What did you mean?"

The second things aren't convenient for you, you toss us aside. How do you have any right to say anything to anyone? In the middle of the fight, Karyu had spat this at Iou. But Sasuke didn't know the details behind this.

"What's the point of asking about that?!" Iou cried. "It doesn't change the fact that they're evil!"

"If you're going to yell, go outside. I can't make any decisions until I know everything." Sasuke's words made Iou swallow hard.

"Can't you just look with the sharingan?" Karyu teased, but Sasuke simply stared silently at him until he guffawed and looked away. "My Lava Style is a kekkei genkai. Although in Kumogakure, shinobi who use the same Lava Style as I do are apparently given important posts, I was born into a small country village. So every time a fight broke out with an outsider, our clan was made to stand at the very front lines. They said that it was only natural to contribute to the village, given that we had special powers. Because of that, everyone died young."

Karyu slowly told the tale of his own past.

"I knew I'd be killed by the village one day too, so I left. The village sent ninja after me to kill me. I fled desperately, but my back was pushed up against the wall; I couldn't run anymore. And then, the Bright Lightning Group took me in."

That was back when they were called chivalrous thieves.

"The head of Bright Lightning Group had a kekkei genkai he was persecuted for, too, just like me. Which was exactly why he wanted to be an ally to the weak. He crushed people doing evil things, and gave the money he got from them to the poor....like to this village, hm?"

Iou pressed his lips together tightly.

"We were treated almost like heroes. Whenever we showed

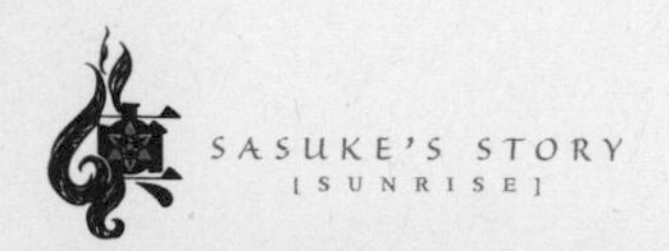

ourselves, the people of the villages welcomed us. They'd give us food and lodging. Good times."

So they had built good relationships at the time. Then how did this tragedy come about?

"Seeing how we didn't belong to any village and yet we wielded power, ninja villages tried to use that," Karyu continued. "They had us crush the source of capital for hostile ninja villages. It was like that then, too. During the era of the previous Mizukage, Kirigakure offered us work. They asked us to go attack the senior officials of a land that was squeezing money from the weak."

This was the era when Kirigakure was known as the Village of Bloody Mist. The face of Momochi Zabuza as they faced off on a mission with Team 7 popped up in the back of Sasuke's mind. He had been a man with terrible bloodlust.

"For us, Kirigakure was a valued client. However, when we attacked the group of officials they told us to, ninja from Kirigakure appeared and surrounded us, of all things. The ninja of Kirigakure, gallantly arriving to save the officials in a tight spot! So, well, Kirigakure used us to curry favor with the officials."

Karyu let out a sigh, like he was cursing their fate.

"We knew too much. They dealt with us efficiently; they also had the ulterior motive of trying to build a channel with the officials. They had lined up their best and brightest. We lost comrades, but we just barely managed to escape with our lives, thanks to the chief's Lava techniques. We arrived here in the village of Takeno. We said, please let us rest here, just for a little while. We had no intention of causing any trouble for the village; we planned to leave soon. The answer came back quickly enough: 'Go somewhere else.'"

Sasuke could feel the coldness of those words. It was more than enough to make a person despair.

"I-if we had hidden you, they might've hurt us too!" Iou protested. "And to begin with, it's mighty nervy of you to take on such a big shot attitude, when all you were doing was handing out money you took from someone else!"

"Such memories..." Karyu replied. "Those are the very words you said to me when I pleaded with you, with my comrade in my arms on death's doorstep, to at least let him stay there, just for a very short while! The door to the village was very firmly closed, and we walked through the bamboo grove to another village. My comrade died along the way, you know. At every village, all the villages, the answer was the same. You wouldn't even give us a cup of water!"

There was hatred in Karyu's eyes. Iou trembled at the light in them.

"The chief disbanded Bright Lightning, and everyone fled their own separate ways. It wasn't as though we had any dreams or hope. Fearing our Kiri pursuers, we lived like rats for who knows how many years... And then I heard about you attacking the summit of the five Kages, Sasuke."

Karyu narrowed his eyes, as if remembering that time.

"I was so moved at the way you lived as you pleased, not bending before the fate of the kekkei genkai. I wanted to be like you. So I got some new comrades together, and formed the Dark Thunder group. Our objective...revenge!"

Sasuke remained silent.

"At first, there were only a few of us, but after the Fourth

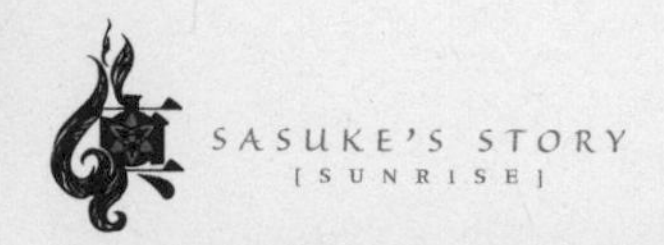

Great War, we gradually grew in number. With fewer battles, ninja were out of work, and they left their villages to join up with us. And now that we have plentiful strength...we're carrying out our vengeance. On the villages that rejected us!"

"So that gives you an excuse to kill everyone?!" Iou shouted. "Some people have nothing to do with any of this, you know?! Why would you do something so awful?"

"You all were living so happily, stupid faces out in the sun, not feeling any kind of pain...that alone was annoying! So we crushed all of you!" A fierce malice bled onto Karyu's face. "Getting revenge was fun. The way your daughter wept and begged for her life, it was magnificent!"

"Y-you monsteeeeeeeeeerrr! I'll kill you!" Iou started to fly at Karyu, and Nowaki hurried to stop him.

"Was there no other way?" Nowaki asked.

Karyu dropped his eyes. "I wouldn't have been able to stand it any other way," he replied.

Sasuke watched over all of this with a bitter taste in his mouth. It was almost like he was looking at his old self.

Nowaki returned the agitated Iou to his home, rather forcefully. The wall of Iou's house was destroyed, and the building was smashed here and there in other ways, but there was a roof and a bed. Iou had a place to rest.

Sasuke left the shed, and went on his own into the bamboo grove, where he spotted a rock and sat down. He pulled out a piece of the paper he carried for communication, and wrote a concise description of the events in Takeno, before entrusting it to the hawk he called with his mind, and sending the bird toward Konoha.

How to deal with Dark Thunder wasn't a problem Sasuke could resolve on his own. He wanted to seek the Hokage Kakashi's judgment. Sasuke had originally been working to investigate the large number of shinobi who had disappeared, but he couldn't very well leave Takeno before he got a response from Konoha.

Sasuke looked up at the sky. A hazy moon hung beyond the bamboo leaves.

The chain of hatred that wrapped again and again around the pillar of vengeance. Wasn't there a way to save people from it?

"...It's not easy." The words slipped out of his mouth. And then he sighed, and went back to keep watch over the Dark Thunder group, to at least prevent any further tragedy.

2

Due to the sudden attack, the village of Konoha was in a state of commotion. They couldn't see a clear motive for the enemy. On top of that, there was the possibility of something similar happening in the future. Village security was enhanced, and a peculiar tension raced through the village.

After she had used Mind Transmission to save Aoba from the genjutsu trap, the damage to Ino was greater than expected, and she was in the hospital for several days.

Sasuke and Choji bought fruit, and went to her hospital room to pay a visit to their childhood friend.

"Oh? Sai?" When they went inside, they found Sai sitting on

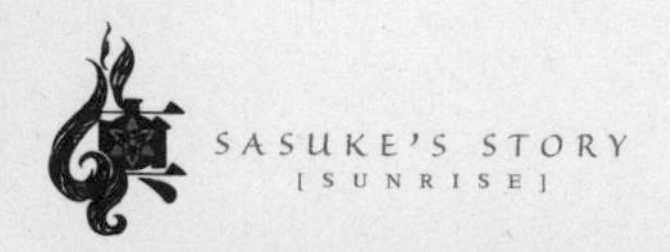

a chair, sketching, and Ino asleep on the bed.

"Hey."

"What? You came to visit, too?"

They peeked at Sai's sketchbook from behind, and saw he was drawing a flower. When they looked, there was indeed a dewy fresh flower in a vase by the window of the hospital room.

"...You didn't actually bring that, did you?"

"I guess Ino's mom brought it?"

"Oh, ohh. She did?" Noting that it wasn't like Sai to bring flowers, Shikamaru set the fruit down on the shelf. His gaze then shifted to the garbage can immediately next to the shelf.

"We're not gonna have any, Shikamaru?" Choji asked.

"Hm? Oh, Ino's sleeping. Just hold on."

"What..." Choji's shoulders slumped in disappointment; he pulled a banana out of his clothes and shoved it in his mouth. Apparently, he had brought some fruit for himself, too. But he had used a secret ninjutsu and depleted his chakra and his fat stores, so it was no wonder he was trying to take in some extra calories.

"But this has turned into a serious drag," Shikamaru said, sitting down on an extra chair. "It's not just Konoha; the same thing's happening in Kiri and Kumo."

The evening the shinobi under the control of a genjutsu showed up in the village of Konohagakure, Kirigakure and Kumogakure had fought similar battles. The ninja who showed up in the other two villages had been a mix of Kiri and Kumo, and many of them had exploded.

"I'm glad we managed to send information to the other villages right away, so they could minimize the damage, but even so..."

They shared information via email. There were still more than a few ninja who resisted the shift to digital, but information that normally took a few days could be exchanged in an instant.

"They said that the mind-controlled ninja were basically people who had gone missing, right?"

"I guess they can't say for sure, though. Kumo and Kiri are supposed to send over new documents, so the investigation'll move forward in Konoha, too."

They had confirmed that Tadaichi and the others were ninja of the village, but they still hadn't fully gotten a full picture of the affiliation for the other villages.

"The genjutsu still hasn't been undone, huh?" Choji said, eating his second banana.

Considering the risk of explosion, the people under the genjutsu were being kept in a facility a little ways from Konoha. Treatment was proceeding under Sakura's supervision, but the medical ninja were still racking their brains as to how to deal with the suspicious chakra circulating in the victims' bodies. Just in case, they had shinobi from the Nara clan and the Hyuga clan permanently stationed there; Shikamaru himself had just come from being on duty there.

"Sakura said she could almost see a way in, though. But I mean, talking about this in a person's sickroom, we can't help ourselves, huh?"

What Ino needed now was rest. They couldn't cause a commotion and interfere with that.

Shikamaru stood up and looked down at Sai, who was indifferently sketching his flowers, not bothering to get involved in their conversation. "Sai, what are you going to do?"

"I've got nothing going on. Once I draw a picture I'm satisfied with, I'll go home." Sai grinned at Shikamaru.

It was a strange thing to sit and sketch in a hospital room when you were supposed to be visiting the sick person, and even more so to say you were going to go home once you drew something good.

But as if accepting Sai's words, Shikamaru looked at the garbage can. Several unfinished drawings had been tossed in there.

After they left Ino's room, they walked down the hall, and Shikamaru muttered, "I just don't get it."

"You don't get what?"

"Oh, it's like..." When they had first met, Shikamaru hadn't felt any emotion in that smile that rose up onto Sai's face. But such an enormous change that had come over him. You never knew what was going to happen in life.

Looking at the evasive Shikamaru, Choji started laughing. "Well, you're like that, you know, Shikamaru."

"That? What do you mean, that?"

"Come on, I mean, you were all like, 'flowers?!', weren't you?"

"You know what? Just forget it." Shikamaru interrupted whatever Choji was trying to say, and left the hospital. As he narrowed his eyes at the dazzling sunlight, a single hawk passed across his field of view.

Shikamaru recalled how Sakura looked after many sleepless days and nights of treating people.

I wonder what we're going to do with them.

The face of Sakura came to life in the back of his mind,

empty eyes filling with tears when Danzo gave permission to eliminate then-deserter Sasuke, and the thought came to him abruptly.

"Was that thoughtless?"

"Shikamaru?"

"Hm? Oh, it's nothing."

∞

The first one to notice the hawk flying directly down to the Hokage's office was Naruto, as he took up the papers that had just arrived from Kirigakure and Kumogakure.

"Master Kakashi, it's Sasuke's hawk!" Naruto raced over to the window and invited the hawk into the room.

"Oh, something from Sasuke? Perfect timing." Ever since the attack on Konoha, Kakashi had been swamped with village business and communications with the other villages, but he had been just thinking he should really get in touch with Sasuke. He took the letter from the hawk.

"What's he say?"

"He's apparently caught this band of thieves called the Dark Thunder group that was attacking villages in the Land of Steam. The leader has a kekkei genkai."

Sasuke had written that he wanted the Hokage's judgement. At any rate, it was in the Land of Steam. It was hard to decide whether to leave it to Yugakure to handle, or to have Konoha take charge of it.

"We'll have to get in touch with Yugakure about this." Kakashi made plans in his head.

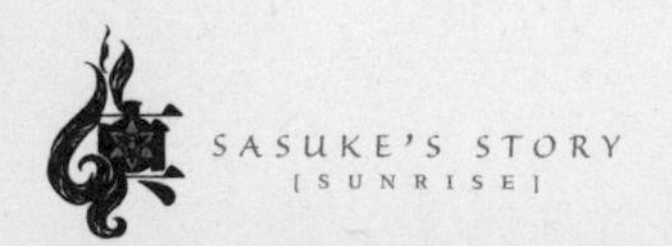

"No word for anyone in his letters, as usual." Naruto cackled, looking somehow delighted. Maybe he was happy with what Sasuke was up to. "Alllll right! Can't lose out to that guy!"

For Naruto, Sasuke was an eternal rival. This had apparently lit a fire under him. He picked up the papers once more and began flipping through them.

Amongst the documents were pictures of kidnapped ninja in this case. In the old days, they likely wouldn't have been given this sort of information. The villages would have hidden it to keep it from being leaked to other villages. Noting that it was precisely now that the squabbling amongst the five great nations had disappeared that they could cooperate like this, Kakashi shifted in his chair, and went to write a letter to Yugakure.

Naruto cocked his head to one side. "Hmm?"

"What is it, Naruto?"

"There's nothing on this one person."

"Nothing? What do you mean?"

"I mean, there's no paperwork for one of the controlled ninja!" Naruto made this declaration, even though he had only just glanced at the documents. He may have been rough around the edges, but Naruto had his clever side. He often found the path to solving the issue at hand.

"Naruto, could you double check to be sure there's no mistake?" Kakashi asked.

"I'm telling you!" Naruto shouted, and jumped out the open window.

∞

Medical equipment had been brought to a facility a short distance from the village, and medical ninja were handling things there twenty-four hours a day.

"Naruto?" Sakura, who was continuing to treat the ninja, noticed Naruto right away when he stepped inside. He could see exhaustion in her face. In addition to being charged with these lives, if she made one wrong move, there could be an explosion, with many more lives sacrificed. She couldn't relax her focus for even a second.

And beside Sakura was another familiar face. "Naruto."

"Hinata. Oh, right, you were on guard today."

"There's that, too," Hinata said, looking at Sakura.

"I'm trying something right now, right?" Sakura said. "So I borrowed the power of the byakugan. Anyway, what's going on?"

"Ohh. I was actually just looking at the documents on the missing ninja." Naruto explained to the women that there was a ninja without any documentation.

"I see. So who is it?" Sakura looked around the room, partitioned off into smaller units.

"Umm." As if searching for an answer, Naruto peeked in on the ninja in each room, one at a time. "This guy."

The ninja he finally found was a man in his late twenties. For some reason, he was in a room a ways off from the other ninja. Hearing this from Naruto, the look on Sakura's face changed abruptly.

"What's wrong?" he asked.

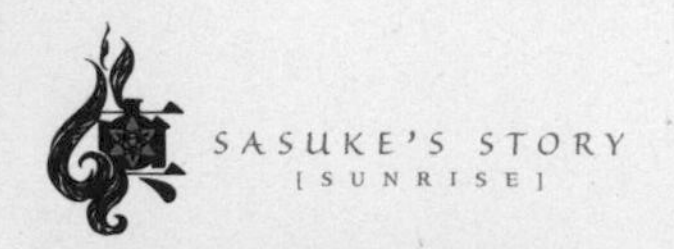

"Compared with the other ninja, there's relatively little of the foreign chakra circulating in his body. So I tried working to eliminate that, and it looks like we might succeed soon." What Sakura was apparently saying was that she and Hinata had grasped the exact location of the foreign chakra circulating in the body, and that she was removing it with medical ninjutsu without making any wounds.

"But that this man alone would have no papers... He couldn't possibly be connected to the ringleader?" Hinata stared at the man.

"Thinking about it, it makes sense that only he would have less foreign chakra... Because he alone didn't need to be controlled." Sakura exhaled as if to calm her mind, and looked at the man. "I'm still going to continue the treatment."

"Got it," Naruto said.

It was Sakura's dedication as a medical ninja. If she succeeded, they might be able to save the other ninja, too. She restarted the treatment, and once Naruto had finished relaying this to Kakashi, he came back to watch over it again.

Beads of sweat popped up on the foreheads of Sakura and Hinata.

"This is the last bit," Hinata said, chasing after the flow of chakra. "Arriving at the brachial artery."

"Understood." Sakura's chakra arrived at the blood vessels inside the man, and saw the problematic chakra. Paying the utmost care to not causing any injuries, she removed the chakra, and then looked at Hinata for confirmation.

Hinata looked through every nook and cranny of the man's body, and then nodded firmly. The foreign chakra circulating within their patient had been completely removed.

"Nice work, you guys!" Naruto said, and Sakura smiled brightly, while Hinata looked bashful.

"But now what are we going to do?" Sakura asked, wiping away her sweat. "Did Master Kakashi say anything?"

"Hang on a sec!" Naruto shot out of the room. "Hey! It worked!"

Aoba walked into the room, now finally recovered from losing consciousness when caught in the genjutsu trap.

"Aoba, are you all right?" Sakura asked.

"Thanks to you," Aoba replied, adjusting his sunglasses.

"But what are you doing here?"

"I asked the Hokage to let me try one more time."

"Try? You mean, you're going to read him?"

"Yes." Aoba probably couldn't just let things stand the way they were.

"Um," Hinata seemed worried. "We've erased all the chakra that was circulating in his body, but the genjutsu trap might still be there."

"It's okay," Aoba replied. "I've already experienced it once, so I know what it feels like when the genjutsu trap activates. If it seems dangerous, I'll pull out right away."

It seemed a little uncertain, but given that he had already gone through it once, it might indeed go well this time. And they urgently needed to find out how this man with no papers was involved in the incident.

"Here I go, then." Aoba reached a hand out to the man's forehead, and sent his consciousness flying inside.

"Okay."

When Aoba got inside and opened his eyes, there was an enormous brain enshrined there. He looked at his surroundings, but there was no red sea waiting to swallow him up.

"This time for sure."

Still on guard, he reached into the brain. He began to see a scene. It was night. The man was standing on a cliff, waves crashing against it. A slender young man stood directly in front of him. The first man called to this boy, "Boss." The boy called boss did not look back.

"It's been a long time since Bright Lightning was disbanded," the man said, almost talking to himself. *"That Karyu, he's made a new group, Dark Thunder, and he's running wild. He's maybe turning his hatred on the people in the villages. ...So we can't actually live on the straight and narrow, after all."*

The sounds of waves approaching and receding. Regret bled out onto the man's face.

"I want to say goodbye to this world already! But...if I'm going to die, it'll be after I get revenge on the shinobi!" The man's fist was trembling. Revenge on the shinobi. There was no reason for a ninja of Kiri or Kumo to say something like that. They were probably right to assume that this man was one of the criminals behind this incident.

"Amuda." For the first time, the boy spoke. Amuda. Probably the name of the owner of this memory. *"Will you die for the sake of this plan?"*

"Of course." Amuda nodded. *"I'll set off a great big final fireworks!"*

The boss slowly turned around. *"Amuda. I will not waste your death—"*

This boy was the ringleader. Aoba was convinced of it. He strained his eyes and tried to get a good look at his face.

But the blue sea spreading out before him suddenly changed color. It wasn't just the ocean; the sky, the trees, everything started to turn red.

"Dammit!" Aoba hurriedly escaped from the man's mind.

"Aoba!"

"Are you all right?"

Sakura and Hinata both ran over to him as he pulled his hand off the man's—off Amuda's forehead and stepped back, almost running away.

"It was another genjutsu trap... To read anything further is going to be hard without taking a lot of time and effort... But this time, I did get something."

"Really?! Do you know who the enemy is?!"

"This guy's name is Amuda," Aoba said, getting his breathing under control. "He wants revenge on the shinobi."

"Revenge on the shinobi?"

"Yeah."

So was that why he had attacked the village?

"And his boss was there. I guess they used to be in an organization called Bright Lightning."

"Bright Lightning...I wonder if we can find any information on them."

"Also," Aoba continued, "their comrades who broke away are working under the name Dark Thunder."

"Dark Thunder?!" Naruto shouted, involuntarily.

"What? Do you know them?"

"No, not really."

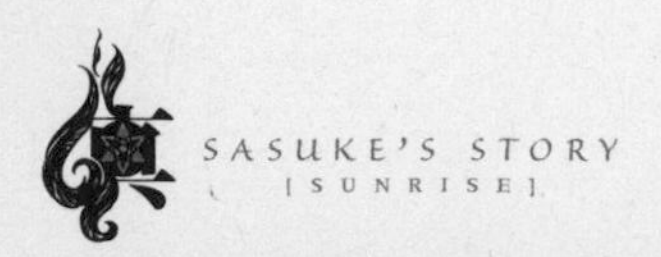

A blue vein popped up on Sakura's forehead. "What? You got our hopes up and everything!" she shouted, brandishing a fist.

"No, but I mean, I've, like, heard that name somewhere." Naruto pushed his index finger firmly against his forehead, and tried to remember.

"Naruto...Was someone talking to you about Dark Thunder?" Hinata asked, timidly.

Naruto gasped, suddenly finding the thread of the memory. "Sasuke!"

"Huh?! What's Sasuke got to do with it?!"

"Sasuke's letter! Sasuke's hawk arrived at Master Kakashi's, and in the letter, he wrote something about taking down this group of thieves called Dark Thunder!"

3

In the attack by the Dark Thunder Group, many of the people of the village of Takeno had been injured and lost their homes, but those who could move were working hard at rebuilding. Using the bamboo growing in abundance around them, they mended the holes Karyu's attack had made in their homes. Having had a taste of the terror of death, they were simply grateful to be alive at that point.

In the middle of all this, Iou stayed locked up in his house, refusing to come out.

The sun was setting and the villagers were turning in for

the day when Sasuke checked in on the shed where the Dark Thunder members were being held to make sure nothing was out of the ordinary.

"You look like you're not happy about something. You okay?" Chino asked. Having been dragged into this incident, Chino and Nowaki were staying in the village and helping with the recovery.

He didn't bother to answer her.

"You ignoring me again?" Chino shook her head from side to side, with a roll of her eyes, and tossed something toward him. Wondering what it was, he caught it, and found a rice ball in his hand.

"Nowaki told me to come give one to you." Her business there finished, Chino waved a hand and turned around.

"Hey!"

"My name is not 'hey'!" Chino turned around angrily.

"Tell him thanks," Sasuke said.

Chino looked momentarily puzzled, but then replied, "Roger."

Once she had left, Sasuke pressed a hand to his own face. Did he really look troubled? He slipped out through the bamboo grove to put some distance between himself and the village, and slumped down against the trunk of a tree with thick roots entangled in the ground.

This incident had given him pause. Karyu said he formed Dark Thunder after seeing Sasuke. People in this world were modeling themselves after dark Sasuke, and running around doing evil things. This was perhaps another link in the chain of hatred.

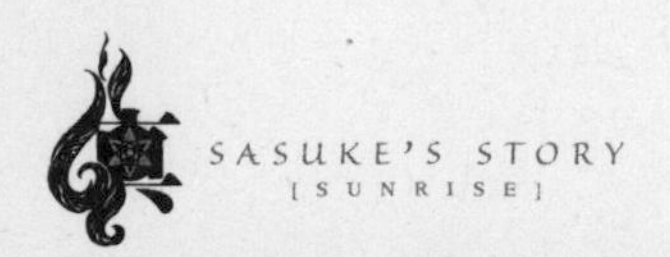

Atonement—a journey to atone for his sins. However, once you made a mistake, perhaps you could spend your whole life trying and still never be able to atone for it.

Konohagakure popped up in the back of his mind. But he couldn't envision a Sasuke who could set foot on Konoha soil and live there. Perhaps this journey would never end.

∞

"Girl."

Iou showed himself from where he had been hiding deep inside the house after Chino returned, sat down, and started talking with Nowaki.

"You sure you should be up, old man?"

"...What's going to happen to them?"

"Them?"

"Dark Thunder...Karyu's punishment." Iou seemed to be able to think of nothing else.

Nowaki looked at him apologetically. "After the Fourth Great Ninja War, there are fewer big battles, and the shinobi of the five great nations are also more lenient in all kinds of ways. And one of these, Konohagakure...I hear Sasuke's village is compassionate."

"It's hard to say for sure, but you can kinda sympathize with Karyu's situation as a ninja... And Kirigakure is also involved, so..." Chino shrugged.

"They're not going to kill him?" For Iou, this single point was crucial.

"Probably not," Chino answered, vaguely.

"...They're not..." Iou was silent for a moment. "I'm going to go get some air," he said, and walked out of the house.

∞

"Hm?" Taking a break in the bamboo grove, Sasuke heard the familiar sound of a bird's wings flapping and lifted his face. The hawk he had sent to Konoha was returning. Had they decided on how to handle Dark Thunder? "No, it's too soon for that."

After the bird settled on his shoulder, Sasuke took the letter from it. And then he checked what it said. "What?!"

The letter noted the attack on Konohagakure; the fact that the matter of the missing ninja from the other day was involved; the fact that among the attackers, there was a ninja thought to be one of the people who planned the attack; also, the fact that this ninja previously belonged to an organization called Bright Lightning, and that he knew a man called Karyu of Dark Thunder.

"Bright Lightning...That's the name of the group of chivalrous thieves Karyu was in originally." There was a strong possibility that the leader of that Bright Lightning Group was the ringleader behind the current attacks. Thus, Konoha wanted him to tell them about Karyu and Dark Thunder. If he used the sharingan, he could easily get the information they needed.

What concerned him was the genjutsu used on the ninja, and the explosions. Over one hundred ninja under the genjutsu had appeared at Konoha, Kiri, and Kumo. Controlling that many people at once was no ordinary feat. One of the conspirators, Amuda, had been part of it, but that was probably a

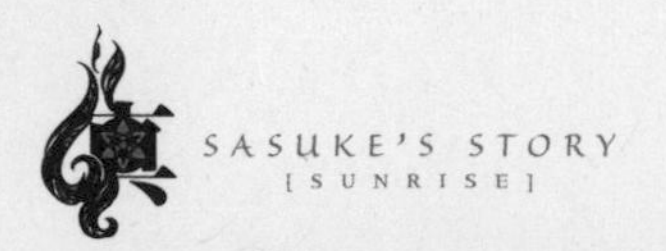

persuasive-type technique. He had no doubt that there had been a ninja like Amuda among the attackers at both Kiri and Kumo as well, but they had exploded early on. Mixing ninja from the village and ninja from other villages was likely a device to prevent that irregularity from being noticed. They had been able to find it in Konoha because they had been able to save all the ninja under the genjutsu except the Konoha shinobi.

Genjutsu and a joining technique. What jutsu had they used exactly? Did this mean that the ninja they caught had somehow changed his own troops and sent them off?

Sasuke gasped. It was almost like Kaguya. The image of White Zetsu connected to the divine tree came back to life in his mind. "No, maybe I'm overthinking this..."

At the moment, at any rate, he had to get information on Bright Lightning from Karyu. Sasuke immediately stood up and then cocked his head to one side.

He heard a *bang*, like something popping. When he looked, he could see flames licking up into the sky from the village. Karyu and his men couldn't possible have escaped from the shed, could they? He raced back to Takeno.

"...This." But the sight spreading out before his eyes was different from the one he had imagined.

The village shed was on fire. Perhaps it had been doused in oil; pillars of flame rose up, surrounding the shed. The bamboo used for the shed heated up and split with successive *bang*s and *pop*s.

Sasuke caught sight of Chino and Nowaki staring up at the burning shed, at a complete loss, and raced over to them. "What's going on?!"

"S-Sassy." Chino got a pained look on her face. "While we weren't looking, old man Iou apparently set fire to the place."

"What... Where's Iou?"

"Probably with them." Chino indicated the shed.

So Iou had gone into the shed, poured oil all over, and set fire to the whole thing, himself alongside them?

"He asked about Dark Thunder's punishment," Chino murmured. "He asked if they would be killed. And I said Konoha was kind to ninja, so they maybe wouldn't kill Karyu..."

Sasuke bit his lip hard and stared at the shed.

It was already too late to do anything.

∞

They finally managed to put the fire out, and he checked inside, but the bodies were in such a state that he couldn't tell which was Karyu and which was Iou.

"I should have killed all the members of Dark Thunder," Chino said, looking down on the charred corpses.

These words cast a dark shadow over Sasuke's heart.

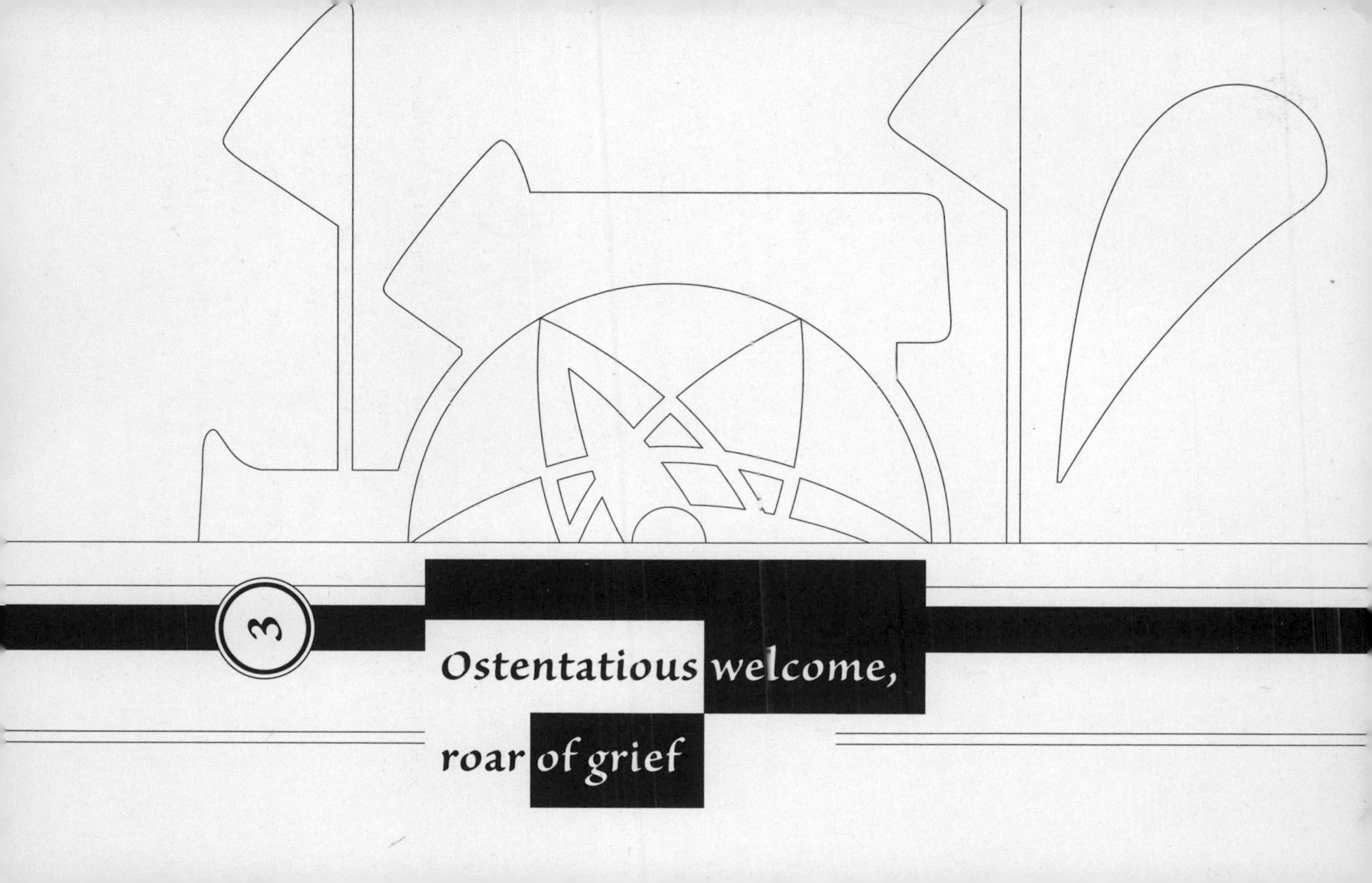
3
Ostentatious welcome,
roar of grief

CHAPTER 3

Ostentatious welcome, roar of grief

1

The Bright Lightning Group of which Karyu had been a member; he had said they had taken requests from ninja villages. For the villages, this was a connection with darkness. When they had dirty work, they needed someone in the know.

Alone, Sasuke headed toward the base set up in a cave, away from the eyes of people. The village of Takeno had seemed relieved somehow after the fire. The members of Dark Thunder had tormented them, and now they were all dead. And it was the village headman who had achieved this. Perhaps everyone was a little glad Iou had succeeded in getting his revenge.

Just as Kakashi had sent a letter to Sasuke, he had also apparently sent one to Yugakure. He must have asked for support for Takeno, since Yugakure ninja had appeared to help with the rebuilding. Meanwhile, Chino and Nowaki said they were finally free; they returned to their travels, and Sasuke was here.

"Well, here's some trouble." A man suddenly stood blocking Sasuke's way to the base. His face was familiar. "Sasuke, right? How about we call me 'Yamato?'" This man had gone into Orochimaru's base before with Naruto and the others. He had been assigned to be their team leader. And now he was here, which meant...

"So I guess Orochimaru is here, then."

Orochimaru had many bases, but Sasuke wasn't wrong.

"Damn it." Yamato sighed. "So tell me what you want, then."

"I need to talk to Orochimaru."

"Well, I sort of guessed that."

Sasuke stayed silent. Yamato crossed his arms, and did the same. He was likely committed to waiting it out. They wouldn't get anywhere like this.

"It's possible Orochimaru had information connected with the ringleader in the attack on Konoha," Sasuke explained, briefly.

Yamato looked disappointed. He uncrossed his arms and scratched his head. "Did you contact the Sixth about this?"

"I plan to report to him if this pans out."

"Hmm. Well, it'd actually be easier for us to coordinate if you sent incremental progress reports as you went, but..." Yamato stared at Sasuke. "But you are working for the sake of Konoha, right?"

Sasuke held his breath for a moment at Yamato's question. He was working for the sake of Konoha; that was true. He was doing it so naturally it was almost mysterious, even to him. He might not have been in the village, but he was still connected with Konoha. Sasuke knew this feeling.

"Yeah," he replied.

"That's that, then," Yamato said, and stepped aside.

"You sure?"

"I'll report to the Sixth. We're 'comrades,' after all.

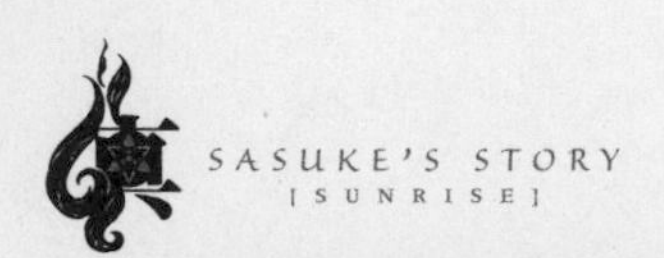

Kakashi taught you the importance of trust and teamwork, too, didn't he?"

Team Kakashi. Team 7. The way they looked back then came back to life in Sasuke's mind. He felt like he was starting from scratch, going around and collecting again all the important things he'd cast aside.

"Thanks," he said, and stepped into Orochimaru's base.

Walls made to resemble snakeskin; snake images decorating every surface. They probably also fulfilled the role of surveillance cameras. Orochimaru was probably watching him. Sasuke proceeded in silence before arriving at the deepest part of the base.

"It's been a while, Sasuke." Orochimaru appeared, a smile spreading across his lips. He was one of the legendary Sannin, alongside Jiraiya and Tsunade, and the depth of his knowledge of ninjutsu, along with his insatiable curiosity, were greater than those of any other ninja. This tenacity touched the abyss of darkness like a snake; there was a part of Orochimaru that surpassed the realm of the human.

"Do you know the Bright Lightning Group?" Sasuke asked, getting straight to the issue at hand without any preamble.

"Goodness," Orochimaru murmured.

"Do you?"

"Yes, well, I have heard of them. But the last I heard, they had been 'exterminated' by Kirigakure." Orochimaru chuckled. So, he apparently knew that Kirigakure had set up a trap for Bright Lightning in order to build its own connections with the officials.

"There's a possibility that the leader of Bright Lightning is attacking ninja villages."

"Ooh, the leader of Bright Lightning, hmm..."

Sasuke's face grew stern at these meaningful words. "Tell me everything you know."

"Heh heh. You never change, hm? I wonder if that's the best attitude when you're asking someone for something?" Orochimaru cocked his head to one side.

"Hurry up, already," Sasuke urged him, and Orochimaru's laughter grew even deeper.

"Fine," Orochimaru said. "This seems like it's turning into something interesting, hm? I'm quite certain that the leader of Bright Lightning is the owner of a kekkei genkai. He was originally in Oyashiro En's bodyguard squad."

"Oyashiro En?" Sasuke was unfamiliar with the name.

"A man who doesn't belong anywhere. He is a ninja, but he's also an arms dealer. As long as you have the money, he'll sell you weapons, so he's known as the Death Merchant. He's quite skilled. He managed to build a vast fortune in a single generation."

"And the leader of Bright Lightning was guarding this guy?"

"He was, but he also supplied weapons to battlegrounds, together with Oyashiro. These bodyguards were the elite; they also appeared on the very frontlines of a battle. Something similar to the Anbu."

In which case, hearing what this Oyashiro had to say would bring him closer to the leader of Bright Lightning.

"Where is Oyashiro?"

"No idea. He has even more bases than I do. It might be quite a trick to find him."

Sasuke glared at Orochimaru. "There's no reason you'd go out of your way to tell me a story like this without anything to back it up."

"I wonder if you trust me?" Orochimaru chuckled again. "That's right. I don't know where he is, but I can lure him out. But that...well, it's a bit of a hassle. Did you still want to?"

"Why do you think I came all the way here?"

Orochimaru laughed again, and murmured, "I feel a draft."

∞

Orochimaru informed him that the preparations would take a little time, so Sasuke was on standby in the base.

"Sasukeee!"

"What? You showing up here, this mean you're planning something bad?"

"It's been a while, huh?"

The members of Taka he had previously fought alongside came racing over to him.

"Karin noticed you pretty early on, and she's been on edge ever since."

"Wha—! I was just worried about trouble starting! Don't just go blabbing every little thing! Come on!"

Suigetsu and Karin, bickering as always.

Jugo watched this little back and forth, and then asked, "Have you been traveling this whole time?"

"Yeah."

Karin stopped yelling and gaped at him. "You haven't been back to Konoha?" she asked, seeming worried.

"So you *were* worried about Sasuke," Suigetsu interjected.

"Seriously—shut up, you!"

The commotion was about to start all over again, when Orochimaru appeared. "You all are being too loud. Sasuke, everything's ready. Shall we go?"

"Lord Orochimaru, are you going out?" Karin asked.

Orochimaru narrowed his eyes. "Just to the ocean with Sasuke for a minute."

Karin and the others were momentarily at a loss for words.

"Wh-whaaat?! Sasuke, to the ocean?!" Karin shrieked.

"Keep an eye on things while I'm out," Orochimaru commanded, and Karin's shoulders dropped.

"I can't really imagine Lord Orochimaru at the beach." Suigetsu was stiff.

"Wait, this is news to me." Sasuke furrowed his brow as he followed Orochimaru.

"More precisely, to an island floating in the ocean. There's an amusement spot for the rich there."

"...And Oyashiro is there?"

"If we leave a little bait, hm?" A meaningful smile spread across Orochimaru's face.

∞

"I can't believe Sasuke would move on someone else's behalf," Suigetsu murmured, with somehow deep emotion, after Sasuke and Orochimaru had left.

"He was originally a Konoha ninja," Jugo said. "It's not exactly for a stranger."

"But, like," Suigetsu insisted. "He hasn't gone back to Konoha, right? Maybe it's hard for him to be there?"

"I dunno," Jugo said, and glared at Suigetsu. "The big wars might be over, but there's still plenty of baddies out there. With those eyes, Sasuke'll have people coming after him."

Sasuke had the sharingan in his right eye, as a survivor of the Uchiha clan, and even the rinnegan in his left. His eyes were more appealing than anything else for someone hungry for power. Just like Orochimaru had once wanted Sasuke's body.

"If he was in the village, ninja might show up to attack it, looking for him. So by showing everyone that Uchiha Sasuke is not in Konoha, but rather wandering around the world, the chance of the village being hurt drops," Karin noted.

"And if he in serious contact with the village, some people might show up trying to get information from people connected with Sasuke," Jugo added.

"Isn't everyone connected with Sasuke, like, super strong?" Suigetsu asked, cocking his head to one side. "It wouldn't be easy to get information from them or anything."

"Not necessarily. If he was in the village, he'd be seeing little kids and things. There are some people who'd push those kids for info," Jugo said. There were still some ninja in this world who would take whatever unjust means necessary in order to achieve their objective. You never knew what they would use.

"And Sasuke killed Uchiha Itachi out of his worry about Itachi being a subject of Lord Orochimaru's research. Some people hate him for that," Karin said. "Isn't it like he's making sure that he leaves as little information as possible with the village?"

"You think Sasuke's thinking about all that?" Suigetsu

seemed half-doubtful of the idea.

"I don't know for sure, but if that's the case, then Sasuke'll always be traveling?" Suigetsu asked.

"He might end up doing that," Jugo replied.

Hearing this, Karin dropped her eyes. In the back of her mind, an image came back to life: a woman, her eyes on Sasuke approaching the darkness, but unable to stop caring about him even still, tears spilling down her face.

∞

Karin went back to her room and took a photo out of her desk. It had been taken back when they were still working as Taka, after Karin had begged and pestered everyone to do it. She had actually wanted a photo of just the two of them, but Suigetsu and Jugo were also in it. She stared at this picture.

"Whatcha looking at?" Suigetsu came up from behind her to sneak a peek.

"Quit it, you! Have you ever heard of a little thing called manners?!"

"Oof!"

Karin threw a backhand at his face, which turned into a liquid, and water scattered everywhere. Karin pushed her glasses up and hurriedly shouted, "It's not like I was actually sitting here wondering if that kid had a picture of him or anything?!"

"Kid? What kid? Sasuke?"

"Sasuke? Oh, uh—Shut up!!" This time, she kicked at him as hard as she could. "Get out, you idiot!" Kicking and punching, Karin chased Suigetsu out of the room. Once his aura had

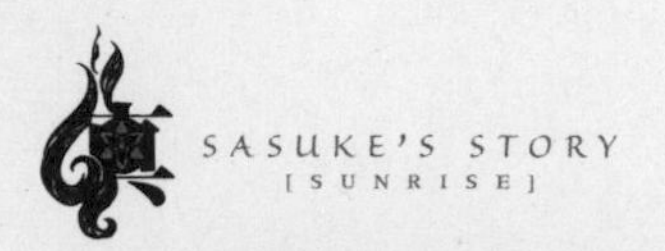

receded, she looked at the photo once morc.

"If I see you again, I can just ask, I guess. It's an easy thing to copy a photo and all." Although she had no idea if she'd see the woman with the cherry-pink hair again.

Karin put the photo back in her desk.

2

They got on a ship at the nearest port. This ship landed on an island, and they transferred to an even smaller boat. The path ahead was shrouded in fog, and visibility grew worse. The boatman, perhaps accustomed to these conditions, paddled the boat wordlessly.

"But it is strange that you can move so freely like this," Sasuke said, staring in the direction of the boat's progress through the fog.

The murder of the fourth Kazekage in the operation to destroy Konoha. And Orochimaru had committed many other grave crimes in addition to this.

"Goodness. You're one to talk, Sasuke," Orochimaru retorted, staring at the waves blown up by the wind. And it was true. Normally, Sasuke would also have been imprisoned. "And Kabuto, he's a war criminal from the Fourth Great Ninja War, and he lives in the outside world too?"

Yakushi Kabuto, Orochimaru's talented right-hand man, constantly accumulating all kinds of things in his body in order to learn what exactly he was. The forbidden jutsu he used—the

Edotensei—had set the world of the ninja on a path of ruin. No one could say he had been forgiven for his actions, the lives he took, and all his evil deeds. There were certainly some who despised what Kabuto had done, and there were no doubt some who looked to his future uneasily, worrying he would make the same mistakes again if they let him live.

"Although compared with me, the probability that Kabuto will turn to evil again is likely low."

"How can you say that for sure?"

"Heh heh. You don't trust the power of Uchiha Itachi?"

Sasuke was forced into silence.

Having been brought back to life by the Edotensei, Itachi fought Kabuto to release the jutsu. At that time, he had used Izanami on him. As long as the subject did not take a hard look at themselves and accept who they were, the jutsu could not be released.

But it was hard for Sasuke to imagine exactly how Kabuto had made it out of the Izanami jutsu, having seen how fierce he had been.

"Look at it like this. Kabuto also had a connection to someone. That likely led him to understand how to release the jutsu."

"A connection to someone?"

"Yes. There was the woman who saved Kabuto after he was orphaned in the war."

Knowing nothing of Kabuto's past, Sasuke was surprised at this.

"She was originally a Konoha shinobi and actually belonged to the Foundation, the elites of the intelligence division. She had an integrity that could almost be said to be abnormal for the

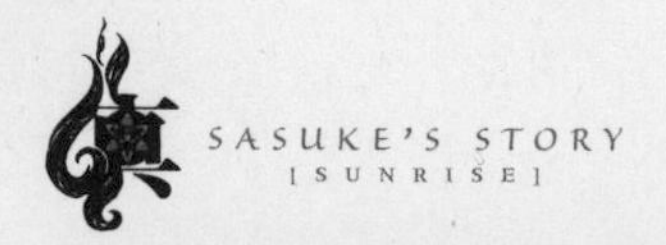

Foundation. But she left that organization and went to work for an orphanage. And Kabuto was there."

Sasuke waited for him to continue.

"Kabuto got pulled into war from the simple, pure desire to be of use to her and the orphanage. The fact that he came to my attention meant that his luck had run out, I suppose," Orochimaru said, without a hint of malice.

"In the end, Kabuto was made to bear Konoha's darkness, and he killed this woman he adored with his own hand. And then he was my faithful subordinate. No matter how dirty the task, he did it without issue. But when he gathered together and used all those famed ninja with the Edotensei jutsu, it was only she he did not attempt to reach out to. Even though there had to have been any number of ways in which he could have used her powers as a ninja. Perhaps all of his human emotion was concentrated in her."

He reminds me of the old me.

In the back of his mind, the voice of Sasuke's older brother came back to life. Those were his words after he used Izanami on Kabuto. Itachi had said that he and Kabuto had both been toyed with by the world of the ninja.

Unlike me, I want Kabuto to realize that before he dies.

Sasuke didn't think Itachi and Kabuto were alike. Even now, he couldn't believe they were like each other. But he could envision that Kabuto had his own pain that only he could understand.

"She couldn't tell Kabuto this, but she had also been thinking of him that whole time. Perhaps in the middle of the Izanami, he had realized these thoughts of hers."

What road exactly would Kabuto walk down from now on? Was it the path that this woman—so important to him—illuminated for him?

"Also...perhaps it's insurance for those times when something nonsensical happens."

"Insurance?"

"Every era has its dissenters. And when those dissenters show up, inhuman powers like ours are sometimes required. Because some things cannot be protected with justice alone. So taming us properly is for everyone's sake." Orochimaru let out a short laugh.

"What?"

"Your friend likely doesn't have an inkling of all this in his head." He meant Naruto.

"I guess so."

Orochimaru narrowed his eyes. "Well...I can see it now." He lifted his face.

From under the cover of fog, an island started to come into view, its outer periphery circled by precipitous cliffs. The boatman pulled into a small cave in the cliffs, and they kept moving toward the interior of the island. Once the sky opened up above them, the dock appeared.

"Welcome! Welcome!" A man dressed in dazzling costume came to greet them. The island was lined with gorgeous buildings, and the people coming and going were dressed quite ostentatiously. It made the heavy atmosphere on the outside seem like a lie.

"This desert island does not appear on maps," Orochimaru said, and they headed forward between the buildings. Soon, a

remarkable dome-shaped building came into view.

"'Arena?'"

"That's read as 'Coliseum.'"

They went up into the spectator seats, and Sasuke could tell at a glance that the people sitting there were wealthy. Furrowing his brow at the abnormal enthusiasm, he watched as someone who was apparently the promoter appeared in the center of the Coliseum.

"Thank you so much for coming today! Glory for the victor, despair for the loser! The rules are simple; just pit your hand against that of your opponent! And then the winner takes both! Survival of the fittest! The very simplest style!"

Things were getting fairly suspicious.

"What is this, Orochimaru?"

"Just as the man said. The people here make the ninja in their employ fight, and if you win, you get your opponent's ninja."

"*This* is your amusement park?!"

Just as he revealed his own disgust, the fight began. A cheer rose up from the excited millionaires.

"It's like some kind of spectacle..."

"I wonder if you remember the chunin exams, Sasuke?" Orochimaru chuckled. "That too is a microcosm of the battlefield, a place where the ninja villages make an appeal to show off how talented their ninja have grown up to be, how much battle power they have. This is like that."

Orochimaru turned his gaze on the spectators.

"They're letting everyone here know that they have the financial wherewithal to hire the best ninja. The rich here are people of the dark side. By boasting of their power and increasing their prestige, they try to make things happen to their advantage. Which reminds me. Apparently, Gato of Gato Transport was a regular here."

That was the name of the man who had once had the Land of Waves under his thumb. Sasuke remembered his despicable nature. No doubt, a lot of the wealthy here were people like Gato. Sasuke's disgust grew.

"But this is basically the only place you'll ever catch Oyashiro En. And he won't show up unless there's a hand he wants."

As they talked, the match had apparently been decided. The ninja who had fought stepped back, and the MC called out the next duel cards.

"Now then, next up we have Oyashiro En's Futsu, and Orochimaru's Sasukeeeee!"

Sasuke stiffened the instant he heard this. "What's the meaning of this?"

"It seems he took the bait."

"I asked you what the meaning of this is."

Orochimaru's smile did not change in the face of Sasuke's annoyance. In fact, he seemed to be enjoying himself even more. "I told you. Oyashiro doesn't show up unless there's a hand he wants. You see, he collects kekkei genkai."

"He collects kekkei genkai?"

"Exactly. He's a man who likes rare things. And you, Sasuke, with the sharingan, well, he probably desperately wants you."

Apparently, the bait had been Sasuke.

"Now that I know he's here in the arena, all I have to do is find him, then?"

"Oyashiro is a deeply cautious man. I have no idea where he is. He's a medical ninja, you see. Here especially, it helps if you imagine Kabuto. It's not an issue for him to hide his form, naturally, or even his scent. But he absolutely must come out during the exchange of hands at the end of the tournament. That is the custom here."

So in order to see him, Sasuke apparently had no choice but to fight. He clicked his tongue.

"Oh, my! Is this a default?" Perhaps waiting for their move, the ninja Oyashiro was playing did not immediately come forward.

Glaring at Orochimaru, Sasuke said, "I'll make this quick," and jumped down into the arena.

At Sasuke's appearance, the electricity in the venue shot up. As if in response, steam appeared in the arena and took on the form of a person. A boy in his late teens, Oyashiro's ninja, Futsu.

"Now, start!"

With the signal, Futsu at once closed the distance between them. His hands nimbly wove signs, and just as Sasuke wondered if Futsu's cheeks were swelling up, something like fog shot out of Futsu's mouth.

Sasuke jumped backward to keep whatever it was from touching him. He caught the faint scent of acid.

"I see, a kekkei genkai collector, huh?" After putting some distance between them, Sasuke looked at Futsu. "Vapor Style, Solid Fog, hm?"

"How do you—?!"

Because kekkei genkai were rare, knowledge of and experience with them tended to be scarce. Most of the time, if someone with a kekkei genkai struck first, they could come out on top, which was why Futsu had immediately attacked.

"I've run into this technique in the past." But Sasuke knew this jutsu. It was a fog of acid that could melt a person. The Mizukage, Terumi Mei, had used it when they fought. She had gone so far as to melt Sasuke's Susano'o with it.

However, this jutsu of Futsu's was not as powerful as the Mizukage's. In which case, he had no need to fear it.

This time, Sasuke closed the distance he had opened up between them. Futsu trembled, as if aware of the eyes of someone other than Sasuke on him, and went to release his Solid Fog once more.

I don't need to show him the sharingan. More than anything, his pride would not allow him to bring out the sharingan in this vulgar space.

"Fire Style: Great Fireball Technique!"

White-hot flames shot out of his mouth. Although the technique was simple, the flames overwhelmed his opponent's fog, and swallowed Futsu.

"Aaaaah!" Futsu cried out at the combination of the fog bouncing back on him and Sasuke's flames.

"Victory to Sasuke!"

Just as he said he would, Sasuke finished the match in the blink of an eye. The people in charge at the Coliseum dealt with Futsu. Apparently, there was also a medical team. They probably couldn't allow any serious injuries.

"Very nice work, Sasuke. Please come this way," a member of the staff urged him, and Sasuke headed into the depths of the arena. Along the way, Orochimaru joined up with him.

"Just like you."

"Mm."

They were shown to a room with every luxury, furnished with gorgeous, gaudy items. The staff member urged them to sit, but they remained standing.

A little later, a man came in. "Ooh, you're terrible! I thought I'd at least be given a glimpse of the sharingan. That's why I took part! I can't believe you didn't even use it!"

Their interlocutor was an arms dealer. Sasuke had thought he would be a rather shady man, given what he had seen in Gato, but contrary to his expectations, this man was quite cheerful. He was perhaps around forty. Although he was tall with neat features, he ruined that with sunglasses of a strange design.

"You're just awful, Orochimaruuu! And here I was taking part after who knows how many years. Being done in that quickly, well, it makes me lose some real face, doesn't it?" The man fluttered about, whining, before shifting his gaze to Sasuke and smiling. "Hello! I'm Oyashiro En. A pleasure."

Oyashiro extended a hand as if to shake Sasuke's, but Sasuke did not respond. Even still, Oyashiro smiled like he was having a good time.

"Is this guy really Oyashiro En?" He was fairly different from what Sasuke had imagined.

But Orochimaru replied, "No mistake at all."

"Ooh. And now I have to trade my precious Futsu with no compensation, hm? Well then, the contract—" Oyashiro began.

"There's no need for that." Sasuke stopped Oyashiro as he was about to press his seal against the contract that someone, apparently an intermediary, had brought.

"Oh? I wonder what that means?"

"There's something I want to ask you," Sasuke said.

Oyashiro snorted and settled deeply into a chair to one side. Then he urged Sasuke to continue. "Go ahead."

"Do you know the Bright Lightning Group?"

Oyashiro's eyes widened slightly behind his sunglasses. "I do. They came after my life any number of times."

"Came after your life?"

"Yes. I mean, they just hate me."

He had heard that Bright Lightning defeated crooked people, took their money, and distributed it to the poor. But did the reason they had ended up like that lie with Oyashiro?

"There's a possibility their leader is kidnapping ninja, using genjutsu on them, and making them attack ninja villages. People have died."

"Ooh! That really is just appalling behavior, even for Fushin."

"Fushin?"

"That's his name."

So this was apparently the name of the leader of Bright Lightning.

"He was originally an outsider, that boy. I won him here, and he became part of my bodyguard detail. He was supposedly born in the Land of Water. That said, he's not from the mainland where Kirigakure is, but rather one of the little islands around it, you see? The people of the island feared him, so he was sold and sent away when he was just a wee boy."

"Sold and sent away?" Sasuke furrowed his brow.

"Isn't that the way with kekkei genkai?" Oyashiro said. "For weak people, special powers are only something to be feared, you know? Just by being different, you're suspect, people despise you, discriminate against you, and in the end, they try to get rid of you. It's almost like you lose the fight the moment you're born."

Oyashiro's eyes moved as if appraising Sasuke.

"I like them, though, kekkei genkai. I mean, after all, they're strong, and that sense of rarity is nice, isn't it? That's why I bring all kinds together in my bodyguard detail. To increase the level of rarity, I've even had all but one person in a clan killed."

He sounded like a child talking about his toys.

"Birth is birth, so many children push back against it. If I couldn't use my medical ninjutsu, I would have starved, you see? Fushin was a relatively obedient boy, but one day, he suddenly took the other children and ran off. I do wonder why he ran away. I fed him every day; I even gave him pocket money. Well, when he ran off on me, that sort of spoiled the fun, and I stopped collecting kekkei genkai after that. They're just hard to handle, you know? Kekkei genkai."

Sasuke was chasing after a criminal who had attacked ninja villages, but he was starting to be uncertain about who was the bad one here.

"You're a worthless human being." The words came up out of him unconsciously.

Oyashiro narrowed his eyes behind his sunglasses. "But Orochimaru helping you, you've got something rare here too. I wonder if you helped these people out?"

Now that he thought about it, Orochimaru had all kinds of rare experiment subjects. It wouldn't be strange at all if he was taking advantage of this chance. When he killed Orochimaru that one time, he had freed the people imprisoned by him, but many had been sacrificed before that.

"Here's what I think. If you look at it from the victim's perspective, the perpetrator and a third party are the same. All the people who didn't help them, they're all lumped together. And you, now, are going to leave without stopping our little amusement. So? Are you not complicit, then? You can't really say anything about anyone else." Orochimaru's words forced Sasuke into silence.

In the middle of the fight, Futsu had been concerned by someone's gaze; he had probably been afraid of Orochimaru.

After thinking for a while, Sasuke made a decision.

"What kind of condition is your Futsu in?"

"Thanks to you, his life is in no danger."

"So then, let me fight him again. I used my victory on information this time. I'll win one more time, and liberate Futsu from your hands."

Orochimaru had been sitting settled deep in his seat, but now he leaned forward. "Oh?"

"And the ones in the stands, too. I'll take all comers. Anyone who wants the Uchiha eyes can just step up." Sasuke swept out of the room.

"Oh my goodness! You're all worked up, aren't you?" Orochimaru said, teasing, as he followed after him.

"Shut up."

"Are you really going to fight?"

Sasuke stopped and looked back at Orochimaru. "I'll free them all."

The discomfort he had felt in the stands. That had been from

seeing the wealthy people gathered there, using the ninja not as people, but as mere tools. A tragedy brought about by this environment.

"I'll end this soon enough." So he would cut them loose.

∞

The effect of the sharingan as bait was tremendous.

The rich patrons would do anything to get their hands on it; they inundated him, leaving him no chance to rest. However, he settled all the contests in a short period.

"What are you going to do with all these people?" Orochimaru asked, staring at the seals on the contracts.

Sasuke didn't want to forcibly remove the ninja who actually adored their masters, but he did seek the freedom of most of them. "Yamato's here somewhere, I assume. I'll ask him to get Konoha to take them."

Given that his role was to watch over Orochimaru, Yamato was probably hiding somewhere on the island.

Orochimaru laughed, delightedly. "He probably watched holding his head in his hands at the troublesome thing this has become."

In order to consult with Yamato, Sasuke would have to leave Orochimaru temporarily.

"That was really something! And you didn't let us see the sharingan in the end, either." Oyashiro appeared behind him, but Sasuke kept his mouth shut. "Oh! Ha! Ignoring me! Surely we can talk just a little? As a thank you for you showing us something interesting, I am now in the mood to chat a little. ...

Perhaps about Fushin?"

Feeling some disgust at this apparently deliberate suggestive trick, Sasuke turned to look at Oyashiro.

"After Fushin left my mansion, all the residents of the island he was from were killed. After that, people avoided it; they said it was cursed. Finally, it ran wild, gradually disappearing from people's memories." Oyashiro smirked. "Doesn't that sound like just the place for the missing Kirigakure ship?"

Sasuke gasped. "How much do you know?"

"It's just imagination, just speculation. If you'll indulge me in a little talk of my dreams, I'll tell you where the island is." Oyashiro called his attendant over and began to draw a map on a scroll.

"Does this mean it's convenient for you if I take care of him?" Sasuke raised one eyebrow.

"Fushin's killed all his owners before me. Well, even so, he did become a chivalrous thief, so it does seem that he wanted to be involved with people." Oyashiro closed the scroll and handed it to Sasuke. "There was a time in the past when I seriously wanted to collect an Uchiha. It's been an honor to meet you."

Sasuke snatched the scroll out of his hand. "Once I take care of this, you're next."

The expression on his face unchanging, Oyashiro pushed his sunglasses up. "Sasuke, you should be careful of eyes."

He probably meant the sharingan. Without replying, Sasuke turned his back on the man.

3

"Leave it to me," Yamato said, stiffening up when Sasuke entrusted him with the freed shinobi. "I'm no stranger to this either, after all."

In these words, uttered so nonchalantly, Sasuke felt like he had caught a glimpse of the other man's strange constitution and checkered destiny.

When you make these kinds of connections, you learn about the other person, and the world inside you gets just a little bit bigger. He keenly felt this link, and Naruto naturally came to mind.

Naruto had grown up as a ninja, supported by all kinds of people. Just how big exactly was his "world?" What would happen in the future Naruto was aiming for?

Sasuke thought of himself. About exactly what he wanted to see happen there. But it was hard to look into the future with these eyes that had stared only into the darkness for so long. And as he traveled the world like this, those eyes only picked up on the darkness in people. But he couldn't just stand still, either.

Sasuke left Orochimaru and headed to the forgotten island by himself. He himself honestly didn't know for whose sake, or what purpose. He just had the feeling deep in his heart that he had to resolve this matter.

He checked Oyashiro's map and strained his eyes. "Is that it?"

A small island came into view in the middle of the ocean. There was a mountain in the center of it, surrounded by forest.

Rotting houses lined the coast; there was no sign of human life.

But Sasuke's eyes caught it. A boat anchored at the island's port. Big enough for a hundred people, probably. He looked at the ship with his sharingan, and discovered the mark of Kirigakure carved into it.

"So that's the missing ship." He looked at the island once again with the sharingan. "There."

Beyond the rotting village, in the woods, there was a human aura.

Kneading his chakra, Sasuke got out of the boat and stood on the waves. The aura disappeared, and he quietly approached the island.

First, the Kirigakure ship. He kicked at the waves, and leapt onto the ship's deck. There was no sign of any struggle. Not a drop of blood had been spilled there. He jumped down from the ship, and landed on the port. There were several other boats tied up there. But unlike the Kirigakure ship, they were basically all small boats.

"The Kirigakure ship stands out. Did they anchor it here and move around in the smaller boats?"

He went through the port and walked around the desolate village. Perhaps the houses had been hit by a storm; all the roofs had been blown off, and the windows and doors had also been destroyed. He passed through the village, and was faced with the woods spreading out before him. The forest was hot and humid, making his skin sticky. The trees were twisted, and enormous flowers grew in abundance; the place was difficult to move through.

But he felt the presence of another person up ahead. He

brushed aside the vines, and stared ahead intently.

He saw someone lying in his path of progress in the center of the woods. And not just one person; there were several. Right beside them were two people apparently keeping watch.

His eyes were already sharingan. Sasuke took a short breath, and approached them, preparing those eyes.

"Who's there?!" One of the guards looked around to try and spot Sasuke.

But this was actually good for Sasuke. He caught his opponent in a genjutsu with the sharingan. The man fell easily, and Sasuke leapt over his body to close the distance to the other man, who was weaving signs.

"Ngah!" The man brandished a fist. Sasuke couldn't let it touch him. He intuited this instantly, stepped on a root popping out of the ground, and leapt in the exact opposite direction from the one he had been proceeding in.

The man's fist cut through the air in vain, and punched the ground.

Boom! A huge explosion echoed through the woods, and the fist gouged out a hole in the ground. The technique resembled the Explosive Style Deidara of Akatsuki had used when they fought in the past.

"...In which case..."

Sasuke pulled out a kunai, infused it with chakra, and flung it at his opponent.

"Ngh! Lighting Style?" The kunai plunged into the man's arm, and the chakra contained in his fist disappeared like it was fleeing. The man tried to pull the blade out, but before he could, Sasuke closed in on him and launched a roundhouse kick at his head.

"Hnrk!" The man bounced back against the earth. Sasuke looked down on him, and caught him with the sharingan. And with that, both of the guards were unable to move.

Sasuke ran over to the ninja lying on the ground, clad in the uniforms of Kiri and Kumo. They were breathing, but they were sleeping like the dead, not so much as twitching. According to Kakashi's letter, the people who attacked Konoha had had foreign chakra flowing through their bodies. Sasuke used his sharingan to check inside these ninja.

"None...hm." He couldn't seem to find any of the foreign chakra Kakashi wrote about. Sasuke tried a counter-genjutsu on the Kirigakure ninja before him.

"Mm...Unh." The Kirigakure ninja regained consciousness. "Wh-where..."

"Can you do a counter-genjutsu?" Sasuke asked.

The man, dazed, pressed a hand to his forehead. "Counter-genjutsu?"

"You were captured and placed in a genjutsu."

"Oh, ohh. ...Right. I was on watch on deck...and then this small boat approached us..." the man said, seemingly remembering as he spoke.

"Tell me later. Our priority right now is to get away from here," Sasuke said.

The man looked at his surroundings. He caught sight of his comrades lying next to him and finally seemed to understand the situation. "C-counter-genjutsu, right? I can do that." He moved to undo the genjutsu cast on his comrades.

"Aaah!" the Kiri ninja suddenly cried out as a small chakra sword pierced his body, sending blood scattering. "O-ow!" He

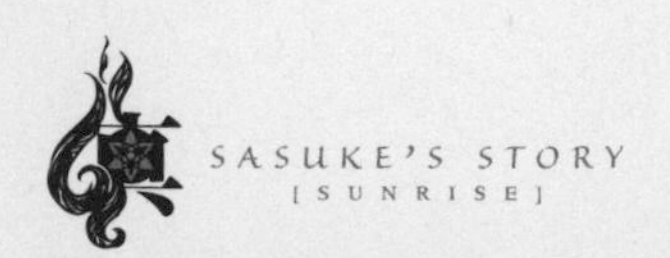

pressed a hand to the left side of his chest and squatted down like he was going to fall on top of his comrades. Someone had thrown the blade at him from behind.

Sasuke felt a gentle breeze from that chakra sword. He had encountered this before.

"I never thought I'd see you again in a place like this." A man emerged from the woods. He had a relaxed demeanor and a familiar voice.

"...It can't have actually been you..." Standing before Sasuke was the ninja he had met in the village of Takeno, Nowaki. And behind him, with an indecipherable expression on her face, was Chino.

"What do you mean, 'It can't have actually been you?'" Nowaki asked.

"You're the former leader of Bright Lightning, and now the one making the ninja under genjutsu attack shinobi villages, Fushin," Sasuke said.

Nowaki pulled another chakra sword out of his bag, putting Sasuke immediately on guard, but he simply cut his own wrist with the tip of the sword. Ignoring the blood spilling out, he cut the opposite wrist as well.

Sasuke gasped.

Nowaki began to grow lumpy and transform. Once muscular, his body now became slender, and he shrank slightly as well, becoming a slender youth, about the same height as Sasuke.

Sasuke stared at the blood that had spilled out. He sensed a strange chakra in that blood. Perhaps the young man had released a special chakra into his blood and transformed his body. So, had he applied this technique to create human beings who exploded when they received an external injury?

"I thought this might turn into a hassle when we met you in Takeno. Even though I managed to kill Karyu, who had a real possibility of being linked with me." Nowaki cracked his neck.

"You're going to spill everything—right here, right now."

"Am I, though?"

Sasuke knew the moment he saw the look on Nowaki's face that the other man was not planning to play nice and tell him what he wanted to know. So Sasuke would have to try to catch him with the sharingan.

Meanwhile, Nowaki brought his hands together and wove signs. A wind danced up around him, and his body was hidden by tree leaves and dirt and dust.

"Wind Style? ...No."

Nowaki also had a kekkei genkai. And the wind grew steadily stronger, with no sign of stopping; it appeared to be surpassing the realm of Wind Style. Nowaki was still weaving signs in the center of it. The wind began to expand outward and grow stronger. And then, finished with his signs, Nowaki shouted, "Typhoon Style! Gale Destruction!"

"Ngh!"

The wind roared. The bodies of the kidnapped ninja were swept up by it, the trees around them bent, and Sasuke's own body threatened to rise up. It really was a typhoon.

"Now, then..."

Nowaki spread out his jacket. Tucked away in the center of it was a chakra sword about the size of a hand. Nowaki took this, concentrated chakra in it, and then casually tossed it. The chakra sword rode the wind to attack Sasuke.

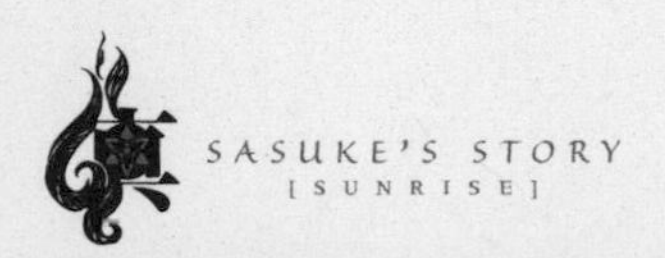

"Tch!" Sasuke clicked his tongue and jumped. When he did, he was caught by the wind and carried upward.

It wasn't just the chakra sword in the wind; there were felled trees as well. And these large trees also became weapons attacking Sasuke. But, using them as footholds, he somehow managed to land on the ground again, while dodging the flying chakra sword.

But the wind was too strong; he couldn't get close to Nowaki. The gale was gradually becoming large enough to assault the entire island. Nowaki was a level of magnitude stronger than Dark Thunder's Karyu, or Futsu from the Coliseum.

Now that he was thinking about it, the leader of Bright Lightning was the one who helped his comrades escape from Kirigakure's elite.

Nowaki wove even more complicated signs, and then released them. "The final blow...Tornado Destruction!"

The rotating winds began to spin in the other direction. Moving slowly at first as if to build up a vast amount of energy, the wind gradually began to accelerate.

"This..."

The wind roared eerily, and transformed into an enormous blade that shot at Sasuke. The blade mowed down the massive trees of the forest, a scythe cutting down rice.

Susano'o!

His Mangekyo sharingan was activated, and an enormous winged armored warrior appeared to shield Sasuke.

"Hngh!" Sasuke caught the massive blade with Susano'o's sword. The squeal of the wind blade and the sword pushing against each other rang out, and sweat popped up on the foreheads of the fighters.

"Aaaaaah!" Sasuke concentrated his power in his eyes. Susano'o heaved one foot forward and started to push against the wind blade, leaning his weight into it.

"Ngh." Nowaki bit his lip and pulled apart the hands weaving signs. When he did, the blade turned back into wind, and disappeared—but Nowaki immediately rewove the signs. "I won't let you end this!" The wind's rotation returned, and a fierce, turbulent column of air once again enveloped the area, pushing at Susano'o; he staggered a few steps.

Sasuke wasn't going to get anywhere until he defeated Nowaki himself. He turned his eyes on the place where he assumed Nowaki was. Then he realized that his opponent had basically not moved at all from before. The center of the winds; the eye of the typhoon. That was where he had to aim.

Careful to keep Nowaki from noticing, Sasuke slipped out from inside Susano'o. He stepped away, leaving Susano'o to keep fighting, bit hard into his thumb, and then, as blood oozed out, he placed his hand on the ground. *Summoning jutsu!*

Appearing with a *poof!* was the enormous snake, Aoda. Sasuke's loyal snake.

"Lord Sasuke, what is your request?"

"Stretch up!"

"Understood." As instructed, the giant snake threw his head up toward the heavens. His massive body slipped through Nowaki's wind, and brought Sasuke up beneath a blue sky.

"Nice work!" From there, Sasuke leapt up higher. The center of the wind. He charged in, and cloaked his hand in lightning.

Chidori!

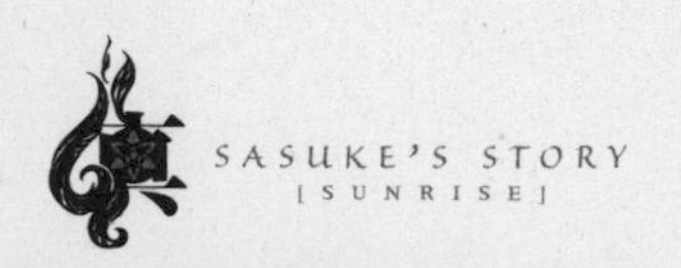

Noticing the whine of Chidori, Nowaki looked up in surprise and tried to launch his wind toward Sasuke, but it was too late.

"Aaaaaah!" Shining with the brilliance of lightning, Sasuke used the force of his descent to slam into Nowaki.

"Ngaaaaah!" An electric shock jolted Nowaki's body, and he was knocked to the ground. The signs he had woven were released, and the roaring wind immediately disappeared. All that was left then was blue sky.

"Hah...Haah..." Sasuke panted from the effects of using his visual powers. However, he had to catch the ringleader, Nowaki, and get information from him.

"Dammit." Nowaki tried to stand up to escape from Sasuke's eyes—but, unable to muster the strength, he fell back down.

Sasuke stood beside him, and caught his eyes with the sharingan. In an instant, he saw a vast trove of information.

His life flowed past like a revolving lantern.

Nowaki was always alone. The great storm that visited the island was blamed on him, and he was sold to a wealthy man interested in his powers. To make him obedient, the man tortured him, sapping the will to fight back. He was forced into unwanted battles, and made to fight for his life simply for the entertainment of his master. Nowaki's power was great, and people kept their distance from him, fearing that power; he was isolated and made hard-hearted by those around him.

He had never once lost. That alone was his secret pride.

And then he had been knocked on his back, limbs splayed in the center of that Coliseum.

"Did I...lose?"

The wealthy man who was his master turned toward the

dumbfounded Nowaki and hurled abuse at him. However, none of this entered Nowaki's ears.

"That's right. You lost." A voice came down at him. A hand appeared before his eyes, reaching out toward him. His eyes slowly moved from the palm of that hand up to the face. And standing there was—

It was red.

His field of view abruptly turned red. He was simply being sucked into a world of red.

"Genjutsu?!" Sasuke concentrated his power in his eyes and forced the red back.

"It really is disagreeable, the Uchiha sharingan."

He pulled himself out of Nowaki's mind and returned to the real world.

Chino was there carrying Nowaki on her shoulders. Her eyes were dyed red. And not just the pupils. Her entire eyeball was red. It was unlike the sharingan, an eye he'd never seen before.

"Those eyes," Sasuke said.

The look on Chino's face became grim. "The violence of forgetting. It's said, though, that it was the Uchiha clan who drove our Chinoike clan to the brink."

"What?"

Chino's eyes locked onto Sasuke. The ground beneath his feet turned into a red sea, and his body began to sink.

"Ngh!"

"Sassy." She looked down at him from above the red waves of the sea. "The ringleader's not Nowaki. It's me. I turned the ninja into human bombs, and sent them to the villages."

"Why would you do that?" Sasuke asked.

Chino slowly cocked her head to one side. "Sassy, you barely listen to anything a person says, and you also don't answer any questions. But *now*, you're feeling chatty, huh?" She snorted with laughter and closed her eyes. A drop of blood flowed out of one.

The drop fell into the red ocean.

Stimulated by Chino's tear, the sea suddenly produced an enormous wave, which came crashing down on Sasuke.

He was pulled into the ocean, and churned and mixed with it until he had no idea which way was up. He couldn't breathe.

"Dammit!" He concentrated his power in his eyes once more. "Haah!" Finally breaking free of the genjutsu, he took a deep breath.

As he filled his lungs with oxygen, he lifted his face, but Chino was already gone.

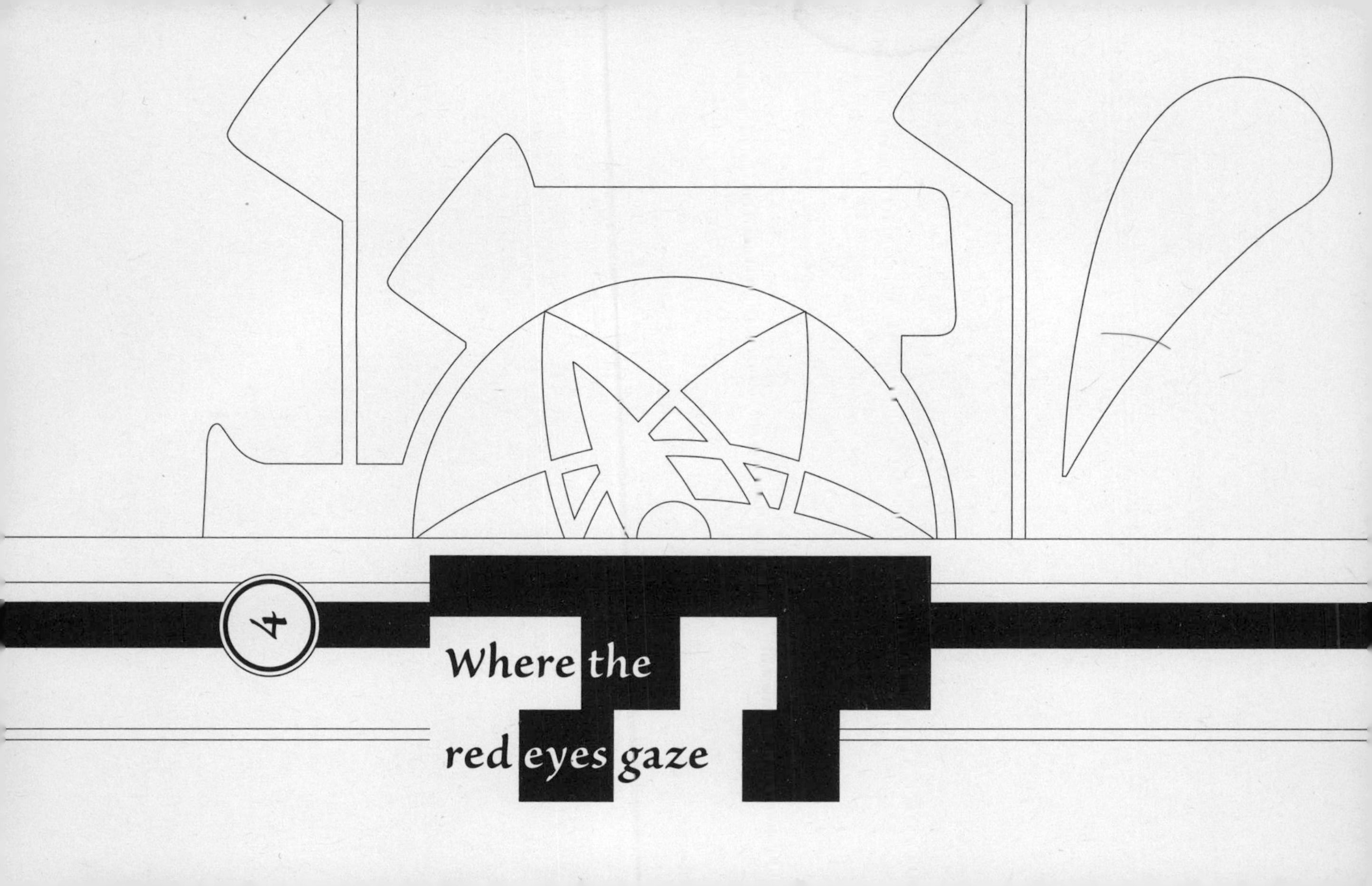

4

Where the red eyes gaze

CHAPTER 4

Where the red eyes gaze

1

Chino appeared suddenly and cast her genjutsu. Before he knew it, it wasn't just she who had vanished; Nowaki and their comrades had also disappeared. The woods had been mowed down by Nowaki's Typhoon Style; the island was a wretched sight.

"Hey, you okay?" But in the midst of all this, he was able to find several of the ninja imprisoned by Chino and her gang. When he woke them with a counter-genjutsu, they quickly regained consciousness. Because they had been blown about by Nowaki's wind, they were all injured in one way or another, but they were still alive. They offered their deepest gratitude to Sasuke—although a little reluctantly on the part of the Kumo ninja.

In the past, Sasuke had attacked the Raikage's younger brother, the Eight-Tails' Killer B, and tried to abduct him. Later, he had also fought the Raikage and taken one of his arms. These ninja adored the leader of their village, so it was no wonder their feelings now were a little complicated.

To begin with, Sasuke decided to take them home to their own villages. First, Kirigakure. Then Kumogakure.

When they arrived at the port in the Land of Lightning where the village of Kumogakure was, there was a bit of a commotion.

"Whoooaaaaaaa! You guys are okaaaaaaay!!"

"Raikage?"

"It's the Lord Raikage!"

"Lord Raikage is coming to welcome us!"

Smashing buildings along the way, the Raikage charged toward the port. Perhaps having heard the news of the ninja rescue, he had been unable to simply sit still and had shown up here. Next to the Raikage, Sasuke could see his close aides, Darui and C.

Once the brawny leader had arrived at the port at something approaching the speed of lightning, he clapped the ninja on the shoulders, shouted "Good work making it back safely!" as if rewarding them. He hit with such force that Sasuke wondered if he wasn't going to break some bones, but with the Raikage directly praising them, perhaps the tension was released; tears sprang up in the eyes of the Kumogakure ninja.

Watching this out of the corner of his eye, Sasuke moved to slip away from the scene.

"Boy!"

However, the shout of the Raikage stopped him. Unable to ignore it, he turned around to find the Raikage glaring at him with a complicated expression on his face. Sasuke looked at him. It was hidden by his jacket, but the Raikage had no left arm. Sasuke's past actions had affected the Raikage's future. The Raikage glared at him silently.

Instead, Darui opened his mouth. "Sorry. You really helped

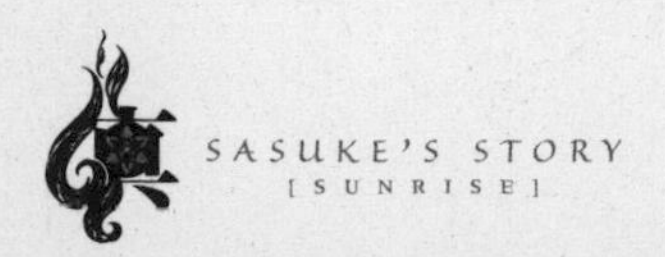

us out." He probably also had complicated feelings about Sasuke. Even so, he offered his thanks as a representative of Kumogakure.

C followed him. "The medical ninja in Konoha say they've found a way to treat the ninja who attacked the villages under the genjutsu; they were able to save everyone. But the treatment requires a high level of skill, so right now, the Konoha medical ninja are on their way here."

In Konoha, they had Tsunade, famed for her medical ninjutsu, and if Sasuke considered freedom to move about, there was probably Sakura as well. *So she's become a ninja people count on, huh,* Sasuke thought. Then he couldn't stop either one.

Sasuke had to find Chino. He set his feet in motion again; he had to stop that strange jutsu she used.

"Where do you think you're going?!" the Raikage shouted after him.

"I'm going to go find the ringleader."

"Then Kumogakure will help. This criminal attacking the villages with such brutal methods! They need to be caught right away!" the Raikage raged.

"No." Sasuke shook his head from side to side. "Only I can do this."

"What?!" The air was instantly electrified.

Feeling the wrath of the Raikage, Sasuke continued. "The enemy has a special ocular jutsu. It goes beyond genjutsu. This ability's still an unknown variable. Considering the fact that the ninja that went missing this time were abducted without the chance to resist, if we approach her carelessly, there will just be new sacrifices."

The Raikage's mouth pulled down at the corners.

"I was also caught in her genjutsu, but I was able to release the technique myself. The only things that can resist those red eyes are my eyes."

Red eyes. He had said it quite casually. But the Raikage's mouth dropped open in surprise. "Did you say red eyes?"

"Yeah. The enemy has eyes that are red like blood."

The Raikage shifted his gaze away as if in thought, and then looked at Sasuke once again. "It couldn't be the Chinoike clan with their ketsuryugan."

"Do you know them?" Chino had said she was a member of the Chinoike clan.

Seeing Sasuke's reaction, the Raikage asked in return, "You don't?" Sasuke couldn't understand the intent behind the question. "Hmm. I have no choice, really. I'll tell you this much, at least."

The story went back to even before the era of ruthless competition between Senju Hashirama and Uchiha Madara.

The Chinoike clan. Living in the Land of Lightning, they had had ketsuryugan, eyes wet with red blood. They were able to manage a variety of techniques using blood. They particularly excelled in genjutsu; apparently, once a person was caught in those eyes, they couldn't escape.

A daughter of this Chinoike clan had married into the family of the daimyo of the Land of Lightning as a concubine. She was a beautiful girl with a lovely disposition, and the first wife was jealous. Unfortunately, the daimyo fell ill and died not long after he took her as a concubine.

"It's because he married this woman!" The first wife then made everything the girl's fault. She said that the Chinoikes had

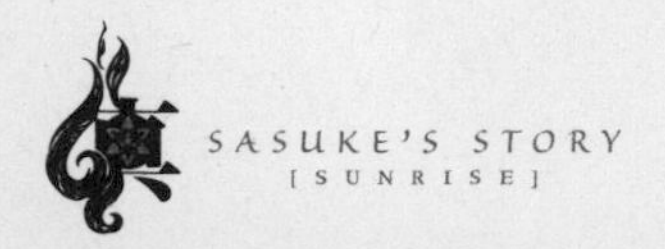

deceived the daimyo and killed him.

It was a just a fabrication, lies from start to finish. But the people around them who knew the strange nature of the Chinoikes swallowed the words of the first wife. As a result, the girl, together with her clan, was banished to a place called Hell Valley.

"At that time, it was the Uchiha clan the first wife hired to chase out the Chinoike clan."

"What...?"

"In every era, the Uchiha name has been widely known. More than anything, the only ones who could have resisted the Chinoike clan with their special ocular jutsu were the Uchiha clan with their sharingan. Apparently, the Chinoikes sought a place to talk with the Uchihas, but they wouldn't listen."

Long persecuted and suffering in Konoha, the Uchiha clan had inflicted persecution on others. That was the nature of war. Sometimes, you chased someone into a corner and crushed them irrationally.

Here, the image of Itachi came back to life in his mind. Itachi had probably seen not only the achievements of the Uchihas, but also the darkness that lay within them. Perhaps that was why, rather than reproaching them, he had taken it all in by himself, carrying the darkness and deciding to die with it, so that the hatred wouldn't be disseminated.

The people involved in this incident now had been forced to bear the burden of the irrationality of the world, an absurdity they could do nothing about under their own power. They were running in the darkness. A crime was absolutely a crime, but would defeating them really end this?

"Boy." Here, the Raikage opened his mouth. "For your sake,

Naruto once put both his hands on the ground and bowed his head to me in the middle of the snow."

Sasuke's eyes widened at the unexpected words.

"It was when you abducted my little brother B, and Danzo gave his permission to deal with you as a rogue ninja at my request. Naruto wanted me to withdraw it; he said he was your friend, and he couldn't just watch it happen without saying something."

Sasuke was stunned into silence.

"Know yourself, know people, don't mistake your path again. Understand what it means that you are allowed to walk freely in this world now. And create a reason for others to accept that." His words were very direct.

Sasuke had previously tried to execute the five Kages and control all the villages himself. He had thought that was right. However, as he stood and listened to this advice from the Raikage, who was a little rough around the edges but still adored by the ninja of his village, he had the thought that if he had succeeded in executing the Kages, he would have been hated by an even greater number of people, and perhaps created an even greater shadow.

"After being banished to Hell Valley, the Chinoike clan vanished from the ninja world. It was thought that they had been destroyed. However, if someone with the ketsuryugan has appeared now, they might have lived on in secret. Hell Valley is in the Land of Steam. The location should only be known to the Uchiha clan and the ninja of Yugakure."

The Land of Steam. That was where Sasuke had met Chino and Nowaki. Also, the Land of Steam was relatively close

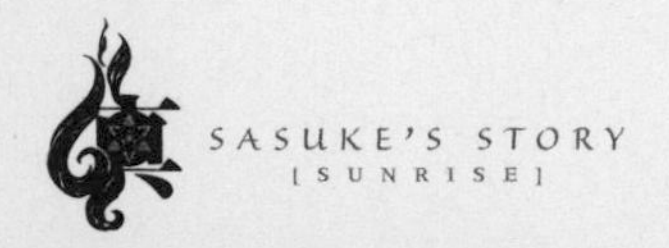

geographically to the villages of Konoha in the Land of Fire, Kirigakure in the Land of Water, and Kumogakure in the Land of Lightning.

Chino was in Hell Valley. For some reason, that was what his gut was telling him. But although Sasuke was a member of the Uchiha clan that had driven the Chinoike clan out, he didn't know where Hell Valley was.

"I'll talk to Yugakure for you. The rest is up to you." The Raikage snorted, and returned to the shinobi of his village.

Sasuke bowed his head slightly at the other man's departing back. And then he stared in the direction of Yugakure and kicked at the ground.

2

After running without rest for several days, he finally arrived in the village of Yugakure, where steam rose up in puffy clouds from the hot springs all around. Resort hotels were lined up next to the steam, and the place was lively with tourists. Because the ninja of the village were there to maintain the peace, people likely felt secure during their stay there. He could also see people who looked to be VIPs of the land.

"Sasuke from Konoha, yes? I'll show you the way to Hell Valley."

Apparently, they had already gotten the message from the Raikage; when he visited the central offices of Yugakure, a ninja appeared to act as his guide. He looked to be about thirty.

"However, the fact that you arrived here so quickly...It will take at least a day to reach Hell Valley. Will you rest for a while before we go?"

"No, I'd like to set out right away." There was no time for resting.

The ninja nodded. "I understand."

Sasuke had intended to go alone as long as they would just tell him where the valley was, but it seemed that Hell Valley was difficult to reach, and only someone from the local area would know it.

"To begin with, Hell Valley is forbidden ground," the man explained as they proceeded through the forest. "It was originally a place that outsiders, of course, were told to stay away from, but even people from the village were told this, lest the calamity of the Chinoikes befall them."

"The calamity of the Chinoikes?"

"Yes." The man nodded. "After they were driven out to Hell Valley by the Uchiha clan, the only path left for the Chinoike clan was to fall into ruin and die. Hell Valley is a rocky place where no plants grow, full of volcanic gases; it's not a place where people can live. However, a few months after the Chinoikes had been driven to Hell Valley, someone went to check on them and saw it."

"Saw what?"

"An ocean of blood spreading out over the rocks where there had been nothing, and the Chinoike clan sipping it."

Sasuke remembered Chino's genjutsu. He had been pulled into a red sea. "Was genjutsu cast on this person?"

"No. I don't know all the details. But after that, the village

declared Hell Valley to be off-limits and prohibited anyone from going near it. And then the ninja of Yugakure forgot about its very existence. They even lost track of where it was."

So then, why did he know the way to Hell Valley now? The question rose up in Sasuke's head at the contradiction in the man's story, and the man lowered his eyes.

"In recent years, someone found Hell Valley once again. His name was Hidan. He later joined Akatsuki and spread the horrors of war throughout the ninja world."

Sasuke never expected to hear about Akatsuki in this place. It was an organization that his older brother Itachi had belonged to; Sasuke himself had also been taken in by them for a time. But by the time Sasuke joined Akatsuki, many of its members were already missing, and Hidan had not been a part of it.

"Hidan was not a man who did what he was told, and at the time, he was still a child. After hearing rumors of Hell Valley, he went and found it out of curiosity. Apparently, he was disgusted by the smell of sulfur and didn't go too far into the valley, but he did say that there were corpses all over the place. So people thought, well, of course, no one could actually live in the valley, so they had indeed met their deaths, after all. But Hidan said that the bodies were not bones, but actual bodies, the blood not even dried. When the ninja of the village went to investigate, it was just as Hidan had said. They found the bodies of people who had only just been killed."

So then, the Chinoike clan had lived on in Hell Valley until recently.

"Some people suspected that Hidan himself had killed them, but it appeared to have been members of the clan killing each other. We don't know what happened, but we once more set Hell Valley as a forbidden place that was not to be approached."

Here, the man closed his mouth for a moment. His gaze wandered around as though he were struggling with something, and then finally, he said, as if squeezing it out of himself, "No. Perhaps we just decided to feign ignorance, not wanting to get dragged into something troublesome. Yugakure has many resources; we live comfortable lives. There is the feeling among us of wanting to get rid of anything that would cause waves in our peaceful existence."

Sasuke listened silently.

"As a safe hot-spring resort, Yugakure has also been since ancient times a pipeline between the daimyos and senior officials of the various countries. Apparently, we took in the Chinoikes because of some connection with the daimyo of the Land of Lightning. There's also the fact that we avoided war with backdoor deals. And by pretending we saw nothing, we were able to maintain the peace."

The man's face was sorrowful.

"It's the same with Hidan. Normally, the established practice is to deal with rogue ninja. But there wasn't a ninja in Yugakure who could take on Hidan. The village decided to let him be. And because of that, people died."

Perhaps a peaceful world dulled the senses of a ninja. And the world would likely proceed down that path from now on. However, dissenters would always suddenly appear. At those times, there had to be someone who could stand up against them. That was probably also the reason why Orochimaru and Kabuto had been allowed to live. But they needed to have other ninja who kept their skills sharp for the sake of peace, ready for the crisis that might happen at any time.

Sasuke suddenly had the thought that maybe that's what he should aim to be.

∞

"It's over there."

After a full day, they arrived at Hell Valley, just as his guide had said. Clouds of steam on a scale incomparable with what he had seen in the village of Yugakure rose up from the ground all over.

"I'll go by myself from here," Sasuke said.

"Be careful," the man said, and left.

Alone, Sasuke set foot in Hell Valley. On both sides of the valley were bare, rocky mountains. The stone face was discolored a reddish brown in some places, and there was no sign of any plant life. The valley was replete with a foul-smelling steam, and hot water jetted out of geysers. You had to make an effort just to keep standing in the place. Banished to somewhere like this, you shouldn't be able to live.

But the man from Yugakure had said that the Chinoike clan had been doing just that until recently. How hard it must have been for them.

Konoha's huge, so you're guaranteed the basics, I guess, but most places are like this. Absurd. Chino's words came back to life in Sasuke's mind.

Hell Valley was bigger than he had imagined, but Sasuke proceeded deeper, as if guided there.

Further in, he stumbled upon a bright red pond. It looked almost like blood. Instantly, he was on guard, wondering if he had fallen into a genjutsu, but there was no aura of chakra.

He walked over to the pond. "This..." When he took a closer look, he saw that red-hot earth was erupting from the ground. This collected at the bottom, and made the water look red.

He looked around and saw that the path ahead was dotted with these red ponds. What the ninja from Yugakure had seen was probably these ponds, Sasuke thought as he looked out over at them.

He drew in a sharp breath. In one of the ponds, he saw a human form. He immediately ran over.

"This..." It was a sight that made him doubt his own eyes. In the red pool, ninja, probably the abducted ones, were snugly packed together. A layer of red earth also covered the bottom of this pond, half-burying the ninjas' bodies. The water was apparently cooler than the earth; he didn't feel any heat from it. But the bodies of the ninja in it were red.

And he could sense a chakra aura in it. With his sharingan, Sasuke looked at the pond and at the ninja.

"This is..."

There was chakra in the pool, wriggling around like earthworms. The ninjas' bodies had been cut in various places, and the chakra appeared to be entering them through these wounds. Once inside, the chakra crept and crawled around their bodies like blood circulating. The ninja with the foreign chakra winding around into every crevice of their bodies had scabs over their wounds almost like lids to keep the chakra inside, and the wounds were quickly disappearing.

Apparently, after the abducted ninja had been brought here, they were transformed into human bombs in these pools, and then sent out to the villages.

Sasuke tried a counter-genjutsu on the ninja right beside him. But the instant he put his hand into the pool, the wriggling chakra started to collect around his hand. A stinging sensation raced across his skin.

"Tch!"

Apparently, the chakra created cuts, and tried to get inside the body. He pulled his hand out of the pool, shaking off the chakra, and looked once again at the ninja sleeping in the water. He felt no intention or will in them. Having lost human emotion, they were merely Chino's soldiers. They had indeed been made to closely resemble White Zetsu.

Sasuke turned his gaze forward. In order to save the ninja imprisoned in the ponds, in order to protect the villages, he would have to defeat Chino.

∞

"This place..." He had finally made it to the deepest reaches of Hell Valley. The scene that spread out before him made Sasuke unconsciously hold his breath.

There, he found a red pond so enormous that the ones he had seen thus far didn't begin to compare, bubbling and boiling, giving off great clouds of steam. It looked like the red ocean he had seen in the genjutsu. The choking heat made breathing difficult.

"Tenacious like a snake, huh?" A voice rang out from a place in the center of this boiling pool, clouded by steam. "I gotta hand it to you, Sassy." Chino was walking toward him, barefoot on the simmering earth. Her eyes were not yet red.

"Why do something like this?" It wasn't his nature to have leisurely chats with his opponent, but Sasuke had to ask.

Chino had been so talkative in the village of Takeno, but now her mouth was clamped shut.

"Is it true that the Uchiha clan drove your clan to this land?"

When he changed his question, Chino's eyes narrowed as if she were glaring at him. "First, Nowaki, now me. Where're you getting your info, anyway?" Chino looked at Sasuke with annoyance. "That's right. Our clan was falsely accused and locked away in this land by the Uchiha clan. Right from the start, the ketsuryugan of our clan was looked down on, compared with the so-called three great ocular jutsu of the byakugan, the sharingan, and the rinnegan."

"But, like," Chino said. "We drank this boiling water, we shot birds out of the sky, we ate the few grasses that grew; we survived. Tired of fighting, our clan lived a careful life here, rather than going out into the world outside. And then, the world forgot about the Chinoikes...or they should have."

"Should have?"

Chino turned sad eyes away. "Oyashiro learned about the existence of the Chinoike from past documents, and kidnapped me when I was still little. Then he slaughtered my entire clan."

To increase the level of rarity, I've even had all but one person in a clan killed. The words Oyashiro had said to him in the Coliseum. So that had been Chino, then.

"This history of my clan I just told you, I actually learned

about it from the old historical documents Oyashiro had. After I was kidnapped, ever since I can remember, I was put through ninja training in Oyashiro's mansion. I was made into a tool to carry weapons on a fierce battlefield; I killed without wanting to. That's why I ran away."

In which case, had she also been part of Bright Lightning? That was Sasuke's thought, but apparently, he was wrong.

"The majority of the bodyguard group I escaped with formed Bright Lightning with Nowaki and moved together, but I came back to Hell Valley by myself. I felt like I would understand who I was once I got here. But it was no good..." A pained look came across Chino's face. "My own father and mother, the faces of the people of the clan, I couldn't remember anything. I didn't know why I had been born, why I was alive. It was empty... It was just empty."

Chino's face grew grim. Her eyes were gradually colored red. "Still, I had planned to live here quietly by myself. I wanted to get away from fighting. But after he was deceived by Kirigakure and disbanded Bright Lightning, Nowaki fled and showed up here. It took over a year for his wounds to heal, you know. He got no asylum in the villages. He had no family to protect him. He had no one to love him. He was used and tossed aside; that was his entire existence."

Sasuke waited for her to continue.

"People like us, born with kekkei genkai, are always made to suffer. Our persecutors call themselves 'normal' and make false accusations about us just because we happen to be alive. They're all 'peace, peace,' but once war is gone, people with kekkei genkai are still persecuted! So I decided to smash it all for them!

There's no hope for the future of a world like this!"

Sasuke couldn't deny what Chino was saying. The Uchiha clan too had been exposed to cold stares in Konoha. That was why Sasuke had hated the village.

But there was a definitive difference between the two of them. Sasuke had been born in the middle of connections, and he had keenly felt those connections as he grew up. Chino had never had anything. She didn't know her parents' faces, she didn't know warmth, she didn't know bonds. That had to be close to how Naruto felt.

You were alone to begin with!! What can you know about me?! Hunh?!

This pain is born from my family bonds!!

How could you ever know what it means to lose anything?!

In my pain at losing those bonds, I yelled at Naruto, who had no bonds, about how he couldn't understand me.

But still, Naruto had desperately tried to understand him, to get closer to Sasuke's heart. He thought about it now. About how painful it must have been for Naruto to have no connections. About the terror of not having a single being to affirm you, of there being no one to love you. And then how tremendous was the loneliness when you found important people from that state of nothing, built connections, and then lost those connections? Sasuke's heart hurt.

Even so, Naruto had never abandoned him, right up to the very end.

"I was jealous of you, Sasuke." Chino stared at him. "Being born in Konoha, bearing the Uchiha name, and having a family that loved you. You became infamous after you left your vil-

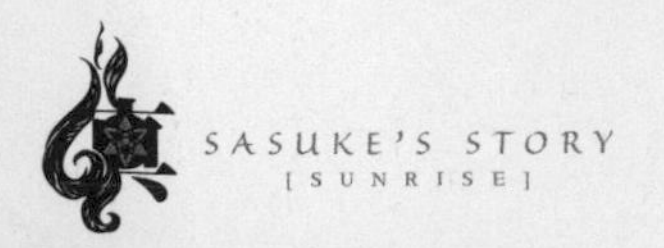

lage, but now you're traveling freely like this. That's because you have people who love and protect you."

He gasped. The red ketsuryugan.

A tear spilled out of one of them. "I get it. That you lived always, always, always loved by someone. You just didn't realize it, you just didn't bother to look at it; there were always people like that around you. Unlike...me." Chino punctuated this with, "That's too much talk. If you want to stop me, go ahead and kill me. But this time, don't forget the ketsuryugan of the Chinoike clan!"

Chino pulled out a kunai and quickly cut both of her wrists. Hot blood spilled out, pouring into the simmering red pool.

"Using blood, the Chinoike clan can make use of all kinds of techniques. In particular, we can use the iron in blood. And in this place."

Chino's chakra wriggled around in the red pool.

"These red pools contain a lot of iron, which further enhances the Chinoike powers."

Chino wove signs.

"Ketsuryugan! Blood Dragon Ascension!"

The chakra squirming around in the red pool began to collect at her feet and rise up, transforming into a red dragon with eight heads. It was big enough that he had to look up at it.

"Take this!" One of the dragon's heads opened its mouth wide and came at Sasuke.

"Ngh!" This wasn't an opponent he could go up against with naked flesh. Sasuke concentrated his power in his eyes.

Susano'o!

The armored warrior appeared, and Sasuke thrust Susano'o's

sword at the head of the blood dragon. He had no sooner watched the force of it send the head flying, than another head grew up to take its place. And this bit down on Susano'o, stopping his movements. Steam sizzled up from the place where the dragon's teeth were locked on. The dragon's other heads also coiled around Susano'o.

Sasuke spread Susano'o's wings, and escaped into the sky.

"As if I'm letting you get away!" Chino opened her eyes wide, as if to catch hold of Sasuke.

Sasuke's vision was dyed red. Chino's genjutsu. The instant he tried to undo the genjutsu, one head charged, stretching out toward Susano'o's wings. Sasuke plunged his sword into the open maw of the dragon, and it ripped through the blood dragon's throat. One of the heads bounced back and scattered everywhere.

Sasuke brought Susano'o back down to the ground. and aimed with his sword at the base of the eight heads. "There!"

His sword pierced the dragon deeply, and two of the heads fell into the red pond, waves of water splashing up high.

As Susano'o and the blood dragon drew ever closer to each other, Sasuke met Chino's eyes, and caught her in a genjutsu as well.

"Tch!"

But Chino apparently had set up any number of genjutsu guards in her mind; several red walls stood in his way, blocking Sasuke's entry. The walls melted, and became waves crashing down on him.

"Genjutsu trap, huh?" The waves touched his body, and his memory was slightly exposed to her. Chino's genjutsu was clever. And his head was spinning. She was probably fiddling with the iron in his body. It would be to his disadvantage to let this draw on. He focused on figuring out how to defeat her.

"Why?!" she suddenly cried out at him. "Why are you fighting for the sake of Konoha?!"

Perhaps she had seen something when she touched Sasuke's memories.

"Konoha's leaves are bright, its roots are dark! There is light and darkness in Konoha! For Konoha's nourishment, your entire clan was absorbed by its roots! So how can you fight for Konoha?! How can you not be pessimistic about Konoha's future?!"

Sasuke got some distance from Chino and looked at her. Why did he fight for Konoha? He found the answer surprisingly fast. "Because I'm alive."

"What does that mean?!"

Sasuke remembered. The sunrise he had seen with Naruto in the Valley of the End. The day he acknowledged defeat.

"I have a friend who saved me. A friend who can share my pain."

"A friend who can share your pain..."

"And a heart that wishes that someday the whole world could be like that too...connects me to Konoha!!"

He would endure until that day came. He would be the one to watch it happen.

I am not alone anymore!

"I'll sever the chain of vengeance running rampant in this world! Just like my brother did, I'll support this world from the shadows, along with," Sasuke spat it out clearly, "the light this world is gazing at up ahead!"

He opened his eyes. This time, the Mangekyo sharingan caught hold of Chino.

"Ngh, ah…" Chino and the blood dragon stopped moving.

Sasuke aimed Susano'o's sword at her. He would decide this battle.

"Chino!!" Nowaki called, and came flying in.

Typhoon Style! Tornado Destruction!!

Instantly, the wind rose up, and became a sword to knock away Susano'o's blade. Although the sword's trajectory was off, the pressure wave sent the two ninja flying; having lost its chakra, the blood dragon splashed into nothing.

"Ow…" After slamming into a rock wall, Chino stood up, pressing a hand against her back.

Nowaki had fallen very near her, and he was more seriously injured than Chino.

"Nowaki! Why did you come out?!" Chino grew pale and raced over to him. Nowaki forced himself to his feet and pushed Chino behind him.

Sasuke stood before them. He looked at the two of them and said to Chino, "You should understand the meaning of what I said now."

Chino eyes widened, and she looked at Nowaki with a gasp.

I have a friend who saved me. A friend who can share my pain…

"I'm not alone. I have connections and live in this world."

Tears spilled from Chino's eyes. Red tears. They rolled down her cheeks, and fell to the ground.

"Nowaki, that's enough," she said, pushing back a groan. "That's enough…" She placed a hand on Nowaki's back, and looked up at Sasuke. "I wish we'd never met you in Takeno.

Then I could've hated you whole-heartedly."

Belying her words, the expression on her face was clear somehow. "I mean, once I met you and talked with you, it turns out you're not really the kind of opponent you can hate."

You meet people and become connected to each other by talking and getting to know each other. Many things are changed by a single word alone.

"You win." Her red tears changed into transparent water. "With a guy like you in it, I want to see what kind of future's coming for this world."

3

Chino stood in front of a red pond. Sasuke watched from behind.

"Sasuke, I saw just a little of your memory. Something that could turn into the answer to your questions might be here." There was already no will to fight left in her. She intended to accept whatever punishment was meted out.

Telling him that she wanted to talk with him before that, she had brought him to the pond where the shinobi lay. She reached a hand in and the wriggling chakra returned to her, including the chakra circulating in the ninja' bodies.

"During the Fourth Great Ninja War, a suspicious group passed under Yugakure," she told him, a faraway look in her eyes, as if remembering it. "I was able to get the information from the mineral springs. When the strange group touched the mineral springs in the earth, the information flowed into it."

It had likely been the White Zetsu.

"I used that structure as a reference to create this technique. But there was something I thought was weird while I was making it." When Chino placed her hand on the bottom of the pool, the boiling geyser stopped and returned to inside the earth. The water of the pond pulled back, finally releasing the bodies of the ninja. She looked back at Sasuke. "In the middle of that strange group, there was one person who was faintly thinking that he should be fighting something different. Or maybe it's not like he was thinking about it. Maybe the idea had been planted in him."

"What do you mean?" As Sasuke listened to her, his heart had started to pound a little faster. He had a bad feeling.

"I don't know exactly. But I feel like they were prepared for something different. To fight a more powerful something," Chino said.

Sasuke closed his eyes tightly—this was the thing that had bothered him in the fight with Kaguya. Why, despite the fact that Kaguya was so strong, had she created the corps of White Zetsu and prepared for war? An absurd fear was about to become reality.

"That something's definitely going to come along one day," Chino noted.

"The idea that there's a being that could threaten even Kaguya....and it's going to appear in this land?" Did that mean that the day was coming when the peace they had finally obtained would be disturbed? Was the future people were walking toward now going to be destroyed once more?

But Sasuke shook his head no. He wouldn't let that happen.

He would protect it himself.

Chino looked at Sasuke. "You shouldn't carry it all by yourself, you know."

When he looked at her, Chino was smiling.

"You have a friend to share your pain with, right?"

These words instantly shut him up, and finally, he nodded quietly. "I guess I do."

Right. He wasn't alone.

Epilogue

EPILOGUE

The village of Konohagakure, full of life, bustling with all kinds of people coming and going. Chino and her comrades had been sent to a detention center in its shadow. They didn't know what punishment would be handed down, but they were ready to accept it.

This group was brought together in one room. Nowaki and Amuda were also there. Just when they wondered exactly what was going on, the door opened, and a man with his mouth hidden appeared.

Realizing that it was the Hokage, Chino's eyes rounded into saucers. She had never dreamed that the Hokage would come directly to a place like this.

"Hello," Kakashi said, a crafty expression on his face; he looked at Chino and the others.

"I'm the leader," Chino said. The head of the village was here. Which was exactly why she had to declare that now. "I take responsibility for everything. So I want you to be lenient with these guys."

"Chino, that's not what we want."

"Th-that's right, Chino. We were there of our own will."

"Well, just calm down," Kakashi said, looking around at the group. "The truth is, I've discussed this with Kirigakure and Kumogakure. And the Mizukage says she wants to take you in. She wants you to help Kirigakure."

Chino and her men looked at each other. The surprise was

greatest in Nowaki and the former members of Bright Lightning.

"It's the idea that now is the only time to stop the chain of negativity. Apparently, the Mizukage discussed it over and over with the shinobi of the village. Well, as long as it's okay with you guys, that is. Kumogakure's already agreed to it. And Konoha, too."

Chino couldn't hide her confusion at the sudden development.

Kakashi started speaking leisurely to her and her group. "What you did is something you'll never be able to make up for, in your whole life. But every ninja carries something like that around to a greater or lesser extent. I'm like that, too. How about you fight again, with your own life?"

Kakashi's words sank in for Chino and the others.

Then there was someone peeking his face in from behind Kakashi. "Master Kakashi! Let me say a couple of things, too!" A man with three lines on each cheek.

"Fine, fine. No choice, I guess," Kakashi sighed, and yielded the floor.

"So, look."

Before he could say anything, Chino said, "Are you that friend of Sasuke's?" For some reason, she just got that feeling.

"Huh? Ohh...I am! Sasuke's pal, Uzumaki Naruto!" Naruto grinned broadly at Chino's words.

"Your friend saved me from darkness," she told him. "I'm grateful."

Hearing this, Naruto forgot what he was going to say and was momentarily dumbfounded, but then he laughed, with a note of embarrassment. "He did!"

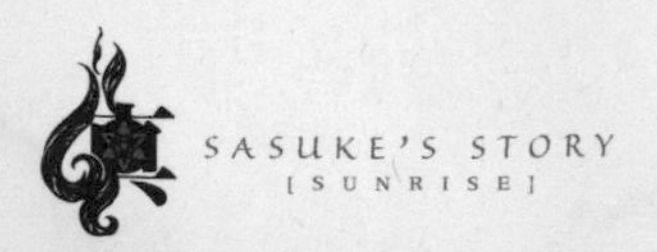

That was the light, illuminating the former darkness.

∞

"So basically, Chino wants to go with Nowaki and the others to the Land of Water!" A guest had appeared at Orochimaru's base: Oyashiro En and his strangely designed sunglasses. "Even so, it's really terrible, you know, Orochimaru? She knew I had a watch set up, and she marched onto the island. Thanks to that, those people were basically all captured. If you decide to catch them all, there are any number of people with offences, you know?"

"You weren't caught?"

"As you can see," Oyashiro said playfully; Orochimaru narrowed his eyes.

"All according to plan, I suppose?"

"Thanks to you." Oyashiro removed his sunglasses, put a hand to his forehead, and quickly lowered it. Appearing there were red eyes, ketsuryugan. "Fights are likely to break out in a small community. You live huddled together for many years, so the little squabbles build up, you start hating each other, and in the end, you're at each other's throats. When my wife got dragged into it and killed, all kinds of things stopped mattering to me. Even still, my daughter was surprisingly adorable. Her parent is a disaster, though," he added.

"What are you going to do now?" Orochimaru asked casually.

"Good question." Oyashiro crossed his arms. "I suppose I won't be able to run arms from now on, either. Maybe I'll turn Hell Valley into a hot springs resort."

∞

Apparently, Sakura's hunch that Naruto was in a good mood was on the nose. Having seen off the recovered ninja of Kirigakure and Kumogakure, she finally had some time, so when Naruto visited her, he happily recounted what Chino had told him.

Hearing this, her heart grew warmer.

It's also a journey to atone for my sins. When he set out to travel the world, that's what Sasuke had said. And he was indeed proceeding forward with a sure step.

But the fact that she wasn't there alongside him was sad for Sakura. She really couldn't wait forever. What if, next... When Sasuke returned to Konoha, she resolved in her heart to follow him for sure this time, no matter what he said.

"Still, it was kinda weird, you know? Sasuke's not here in Konoha, but it's like we're on a mission together," Naruto told her excitedly. "Sasuke's not in the village, but he's protecting it."

"Right. There are a lot of things that only a talented ninja like Sasuke can do."

"There are guys doing all kinds of crazy things, but people who got it together just have to deal with people for real, this time!" Naruto said.

"Oh!" Sakura cried. In the back of Sakura's mind—the person who didn't lose to Naruto and Sasuke when it came to studying—a certain word popped up. Something that had a deep connection with Sasuke.

"What's up, Sakura?" Naruto looked at her curiously.

Sakura smiled. "While you were talking, I remembered something. Do you know it?"

Naruto cocked his head to one side.

"So the thing is..."

∞

His journey continued. Staring at the ocean spreading out before him, Sasuke moved forward at a quick pace.

A presence that threatened Kaguya; he had hoped it would just end at needless worry, but he could no longer ignore it. He worked to find more information to hunt down the traces of Kaguya. He had a lot to do. Things that only Sasuke and his rinnegan could do.

"Mm. Kakashi?"

A messenger hawk appeared, and Sasuke took the letter from it. A neat report outlined the follow-up to the current matter. When he had scanned this, he noticed that there was another letter. He took a look at it.

The handwriting was messy. He quickly realized it was Naruto. A letter from Naruto.

Which read: *So, like, I talked to Sakura. This time, you...*

Sasuke's eyes grew wide at the words that followed. The thought had never even crossed his mind. But somehow it made sense.

This was what was noted in the letter: *You're like the police force!*

The police force. The organization that had been entrusted with protecting the peace in Konoha, with the Uchiha family crest as their symbol. The Uchiha clan had founded it, and it had also given birth to tragedy. But it was a fact that the Uchiha clan had worked there for the sake of the village.

"The police force, huh?" The scope had been shifted to the world, but the objective was the same. Protect the world. And this also led to protecting Konoha.

"In which case, maybe my brother was also the police force."

Remembering Itachi and how he had worked from outside the village to protect Konoha, Sasuke smiled.

Are you going to join too?

Dunno. We'll have to see.

Do it! When I grow up...I'm gonna join the police force too!!

Memories of his childhood. They hurt a little, but even so, a smile rose up on his lips.

Sasuke stopped for a moment, looked up at the sky, and changed directions. "It's been a while...maybe I'll go home?"

He wasn't afraid to be involved anymore. The way forward was set.

Sasuke started walking.

Ahead...was the village of Konohagakure.

END

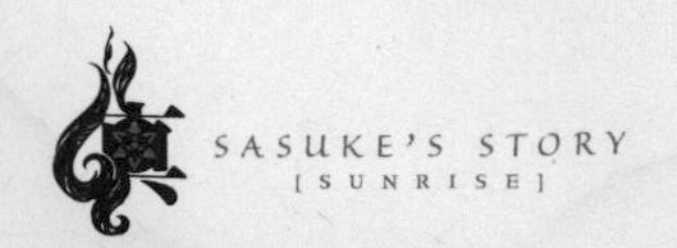

MASASHI KISHIMOTO

Author/artist Masashi Kishimoto was born in 1974 in rural Okayama Prefecture, Japan. Like many kids, he was first inspired to become a manga artist in elementary school when he read *Dragon Ball* by Akira Toriyama. After spending time in art college, he won the Hop Step Award for new manga artists with his story *Karakuri*. After considering various genres for his next project, Kishimoto decided on a story steeped in traditional Japanese culture. His first version of *Naruto*, drawn in 1997, was a one-shot story about fox spirits; his final version, which debuted in *Weekly Shonen Jump* in 1999, quickly became the most popular ninja manga in the world. The series would also spawn multiple anime series, movies, novels, video games and more. Having concluded the series in late 2014, Masashi Kishimoto has kept himself busy this year with the sidestory *Naruto: The Seventh Hokage and the Scarlet Spring* and writing the story for the latest Naruto movie, *Boruto: Naruto the Movie* both of which will focus on the title character's son, Boruto.

SHIN TOWADA

Shin Towada currently resides in Fukuoka Prefecture.
He has worked on the novels *Naruto: Akatsuki's Story, Tokyo Ghoul: days* and *Tokyo Ghoul: void* for Jump j Books.